RIDERS OF THE
RIMROCK TRAIL

RIDERS OF THE RIMROCK TRAIL

JACKSON COLE

WHEELER PUBLISHING
A part of Gale, Cengage Learning

GALE
CENGAGE Learning·

Detroit • New York • San Francisco • New Haven, Conn • Waterville, Maine • London

GALE
CENGAGE Learning·

Copyright © 1942 © by A. Leslie Scott. Copyright © renewed 1970 by A. Leslie Scott.
Wheeler Publishing, a part of Gale, Cengage Learning.

LIBRARY OF CONGRESS CATALOGING-IN-PUBLICATION DATA

Cole, Jackson.
   Riders of the Rimrock trail / by Jackson Cole. — Large print ed.
     p. cm. — (Wheeler Publishing large print western)
   ISBN-13: 978-1-4104-4772-2 (pbk.)
   ISBN-10: 1-4104-4772-3 (pbk.)
   1. Hatfield, Jim (Fictitious character)—Fiction. 2. Texas Rangers—Fiction. 3. Outlaws—Fiction. 4. Large type books. 5. Texas—Fiction.
   I. Title.
PS3505.O2685R54 2012
813'.52—dc23   2012001788

Published in 2012 by arrangement with Golden West Literary Agency.

To
LIL
Who Counts Most

CONTENTS

CHAPTER 1
A GRAVE MOUTH
HAS NO TONGUE

Sunset blazed above the Guadalupes like the spilled paint pots of a drunken artist-god. Orange and gold and scarlet and damask was the flaming background, with highlights of salmon and rose and chrome. Patches of sky like rain-streaked steel showed here and there, their ragged edges tinted faintly as with powdered verd. Shafts of amber lanced to the zenith, paling and thinning until they vanished in the higher blue.

It was a stormy sky. Fantastic cloud masses, pulsing and dripping with color, climbed higher and higher. They were like mighty mountains buttressing the causeway of the stars each with its core of ominous black and its wrappings of spectral fire.

Beneath these sky-flung spires of nebulous change, the Guadalupes stood ponderous and gigantic, bastioned by eternal granite, with mighty El Capitan towering to nigh ten thousand feet in the crystal air. Their broad bases were already swathed in shadow, but their jagged crests were ringed about with saffron flame.

Curving around the shadow-washed bases of their sprawling flanks ran the ancient *Lechuza* Trail — the Owl Trail — so named because it was most often ridden by gentlemen who preferred to do their traveling between the hours of sunset and sunrise.

It is not the most direct route to Mexico, the *Lechuza,* but it has the advantage of twisting and writhing like a crippled snake through the wildest and most rugged section of a wild land. From the flat-topped mountains of New Mexico to the purple peaks of the land of *manana* it sought, and found, a desolate and forbidding terrain.

The Apaches rode it, and the Yaquis, and the Spanish adventurers from Cabeza de Vaca onward. But it is far older than they.

From time immemorial it wound northward, its stones black-splotched with dried blood, its chaparral thickets faintly agleam in the damp dark with the phosphorescent light of moldering bones.

Like some furtive crawling thing of the night, it slithered along the base of the Guadalupes while the sky above trembled with beauty in myriad hues.

10

But the four men who rode the *Lechuza* under that stormy sunset saw nothing of beauty in the flaming sky. Only when the lurid yellow light dimmed and the riot of color faded to watery gray did their lined features show approval. They were grim, silent men, with haggard faces, dark circles under their red-rimmed eyes, a thick powdering of dust upon their sweaty garments. With broad-brimmed hats drawn low they rode, spurring their foam-flecked horses, glancing over their shoulders from time to time.

There was an uncertainty about their glances, however, as if they dreaded pursuit but were not sure that they had it to fear. From each elevation as the trail dipped and climbed, they studied the distant southern skyline in a speculative manner that lacked the apprehension based on the acceptance of grim finality.

As the murky powder of the dusk sifted down from the upper heights and the purple of the evening shadows deepened to the blue-black of night, the cloak of alertness dropped from their tense shoulders. They lounged easily in their saddles, checked their busy spurs and conversed in low tones.

Abruptly one uttered an exclamation. To the east, far across the level reaches of the rangeland that flowed gently upward to wash the feet of the foothills, winked a low-lying star of a reddish hue. Instantly the trained eyes of these plainsmen knew it to be the glow from a lighted window. With one accord they pulled their weary horses to a halt.

"Well?" a lanky individual remarked in querulous tones.

"Think we'd better risk it?" asked another.

A third speaker, squat and brawny, rumbled forth:

"Gotta glom onto some chuck, and pronto! My belly's been askin' me for hours if my throat's cut. I don't figger we got anything to worry about. We come outa the mess clean, so far as we know. Fact is, we ain't got no good reasons for thinkin' otherwise; jest couldn't afford to take chances, that's all. Right now I figger we're okay. 'Sides, there won't nobody see us ride up to that *casa* in the dark."

He loosened the big gun swinging low in a hip holster, adding significantly:

"And the chances are nobody'll see us ride away."

He was right. Nobody ever did!

Chapter 2
Death Sets a Cold Table

The storm which the angry sunset promised made good that promise as the great wheeling clock in the sky said that dawn was not far off. A cold breath fanned down from the mountain tops, bearing on its wings a mutter of distant thunder.

The breath became a whisper, the whisper a wail. The mutter deepened to an ominous rumble, became an intermittent crashing roar. Level lances of rain hissed earthward, drenching thicket and trail and rolling range. The slopes streamed water. The dry washes became foaming torrents. Icy hail interspersed the spears of rain.

Lightning flamed and here and there in clumps of grass or under straggles of brush birthed a ghostly glimmer that was the unearthly radiance from a skull.

The rain abruptly slackened, the air cleared, but the thunder boomed louder than ever and the lightning flashed with a brilliance that from flickering seconds changed the night to day. The winding ribbon of the *Lechuza* Trail showed like a band of molten silver in a blinding flash that for an instant etched the forms of a horse and rider in bluish fire.

The horse was golden as morning sunlight, full eighteen hands high, mighty of barrel, with the fine lines of dainty breeding showing in shoulders, back and head. His hoofs were small and clean-cut, his legs like rods of polished steel. His glossy coat smoked from the chill of the rain, but his eyes were full of fire, his head held high.

Horse and rider made a pair to draw to. The man was tall, much more than six feet, broad of shoulder, deep of chest, narrow of waist and hips, with a length of arm that gave him a terrible reach. His face was lean and deeply bronzed, with high cheekbones and a prominent hawk nose. His mouth was rather wide, thin-lipped, firm, but with a quirking at the corners that somewhat relieved the grimness of the square chin beneath.

His eyes were gray-green under level black brows, with singularly long and thick black lashes. Under his slicker could be seen the outlines of heavy guns slung low on his muscular thighs. The man's slicker streamed

14

water. It dripped from his hat brim. But the wide hat was pushed back at a jaunty angle to reveal crisp black hair.

The rain lashed down again with icy fury, but before its silvery veil blotted out all things, the man saw, far across the prairie, a gleaming point of light. He pulled the golden horse to a halt.

"Goldy," he addressed the cayuse in conversational tones, "over there is somebody who either stays up mighty late or gets up sorta early. Well, folks who stay up late or get up early hafta eat, so I reckon you and me had better amble over and visit with that early rising gent. A mite of chuck and a dry place for a little ear poundin' wouldn't go bad, eh?"

The horse snorted what was evidently meant for general agreement and in obedience to a knee pressure turned off the trail. Threading his way between clumps of brush, he ambled eastward in the first watery light of dawn.

The lighted window glowed to a sickly yellow in the strengthening daylight, but there was no other sign of life about the small ranch house set in a clump of cottonwoods. The tall rider pulled his horse to a walk, eyeing the single light meditatively. He did not desire to awaken sleeping folks at such

15

an early hour. However, men do not ride up to a lonely ranch house unannounced. After a moment's hesitation he uttered a cheery shout.

There was no answer. The ranch house squatted silent as before, with its single open eye staring sullenly through the gloom.

The lighted window was at the back of the house, evidently opening from the kitchen, and the tall man rode around to the back. As he passed the window he caught a distorted glimpse through the rain-streaked pane of men seated at a table.

"Eating breakfast, I reckon," he decided. "Funny, though, no smoke coming outa the chimney, and I didn't smell none as I rode up. Mebbe they go in for cold snacks. Mighta just got in and stowing away a bite 'fore hitting the hay."

He dismounted, with lithe grace.

"Take it easy a minute, feller," he told the golden horse. "Be back to look after you pronto."

He approached the closed door and rapped loudly. The sound seemed to echo in the room beyond, but there was no scraping of pushed back chairs. He knocked again, waited, and got no response. His green eyes narrowed slightly and a concentration furrow showed between his black brows. He gripped the knob with a slim hand, turned it and pushed. The door swung back easily and he stepped out of the rain into a lighted room.

It was a kitchen, all right, but there was no fire burning in the big range. Nor was there any smell of food or steaming coffee. At a table sat four men.

Two sprawled in their chairs, heads lolling back, like men who lazily slept. But their eyes were open. The other two hunched forward, and the arm of one hung down by his side in a stiff, unnatural fashion.

For a long minute the tall rider of the golden horse stood and stared at the strange quartette. He said no word, voiced no question; but his ears strained for a sound in the silent house and his eyes, now cold as the rain which hissed against the window pane, missed no minutest detail in the room. And with a smooth ripple of motion he unbuttoned the wet slicker and swung it back to free the black butts of the big guns flaring out from his lean hips.

Jim Hatfield, he whom a stern old Lieutenant of Rangers named the Lone Wolf, had gazed upon many strange and grisly sights; but none more weird, nerve-shaking or ominous than this upon which his steady green eyes rested. For seated at that inhospitable board beside the cold stove were four men without visible wounds or other signs of violence upon their persons, but with stiffened limbs and glazed, unseeing eyes.

They were starkly, coldly dead!

CHAPTER 3
"ANSWERS FIRST"

As silently as the steel-thewed fighter for which he was nicknamed, Hatfield went through the unlighted house. He found cleanliness and order, and the signs of recent occupancy, but no living thing. He glided through the door by which he had entered, approached a bunkhouse with the same effortless silence, hands close to the black butts of his guns.

The door opened readily to his touch and he gazed at the made-up bunks and the cold stove. Close examination showed a thin film of dust on the top blankets of the bunks and there was a faint sprinkling of rust particles on the stove metal.

The stable was likewise unoccupied, but stocked with hay and grain. There were stalls for a dozen horses, and these stalls interested him. Hoof marks showed in the mud of a well built corral. But due to the heavy rain which was still falling, it was impossible to tell how long it had been since the horses who made them had departed.

Hatfield went back to the kitchen. He was careful not to step on the floor near the table nor to touch the surface of the table itself. He glanced at the big stove. There was no rust on its top, although the lids were cold.

"Used since the one in the bunkhouse," he decided. The condition of the ashes in the firebox substantiated this conclusion.

Next he approached the table, studied the floor around and beneath it with great care. He went over the table top meticulously, his black brows drawing together as he bent low and peered at the smooth surface with narrowing green eyes. Finally he stepped back, the concentration furrow deep between his brows.

At length he turned to the bodies of the dead men, using the greatest care not to change their position, but examining them thoroughly, giving particular attention to the hands of each. After an exhaustive examination which went through every pocket, noted the condition of guns and knives, made definitely sure that none of the quartette had suffered hidden wounds, he stepped back and sat down in a chair which had been placed near the stove.

Absently he drew one of his long-barreled guns with a smooth, effortless motion too swift for the eyes to follow.

Like most men who ride much alone, Jim Hatfield had a habit of talking to his horse, or, at times, even some inanimate object. Now he addressed the big Colt in conversational tones, twirling it about his sinewy forefinger by the trigger guard, flipping it backward or forward with the plain walnut grip snugging into his palm with each turn.

"Five men sat down at that table, and one left it," he told the Colt. "The jiggers who are sitting there now are wearing high-heeled riding boots, three of them, two pairs scuffed by spur clamps and stirrups, the third not used much for riding. Heels are a mite run over, showing the feller what's wearing them did a lot more walking than t'other two. Fourth jigger is wearing square-heeled laced boots. The gent what isn't here any more was wearing house slippers or something like that."

Hatfield paused, twirling the gun by its trigger guard, speculatively eyeing the grisly four.

"Two cowhands, judging from the rope and bridle callouses on their hands. One miner, from the looks of the callouses on *his,* the kinda boots he's wearing and the rock dust in the linings of his pockets. One gambler, the fourth hellion, sure as shootin' — smooth hands, sandpapered fingertips, the kinda complexion a feller gets who stays up all night and sleeps in the daytime.

"Uh-huh, that's them: two cowhands, a hard-rock miner and a gambler. And all four of them, even the gambler, with the kinda callouses on thumb and forefinger of the right hand that come from a lot of practicing on the draw. Cowhands, gambler, miner — *and all four of them gunmen, or all signs fail!*"

He thoughtfully holstered his gun and went out to where Goldy patiently waited, sheltered somewhat from the rain in the lee of the building.

"Well, old-timer," he told the sorrel, "there's plenty of cayuse provender in the barn, and coffee and bacon and canned goods on the kitchen shelves. Reckon you and me might as well s'round a helpin', seein' as we're here."

In the stable he removed the leather from Goldy and gave him a good rubdown. But he did not hang saddle and bridle on convenient pegs. Instead, he replaced them, using an "owlhoot" rig with loose cinches and bit free but hanging so it could be instantly slipped into place.

"Never can tell who might be ridin' our trail," he explained to the bronc. "A wrist twist or two, now, and we're ready to high-tail outa here pronto. Most anything is liable to happen in a diggin's where gents sit down to a drink and a bite and wake up with coal shovels in their hands."

Hatfield made a fire in the kitchen stove and cooked a satisfying meal, which he spread on a table in the adjoining room, the general living room of the ranch house, which was comfortably furnished and had windows on three sides.

He ate in leisurely fashion, with the enjoyment of a man who has often found good food scarce. As he ate, his gaze was constantly focusing on one or another of the rain-streaked windows. The dead men sitting stonily at their bare board in the nearby kitchen apparently troubled him not at all.

Finally he rolled a cigarette with the slim fingers of his left hand and smoked in the same leisurely fashion in which he had consumed his meal, his glance still following the triple windows. Casually he pinched out the butt and placed it neatly on a saucer. Then he stood up, loosened the big guns in their carefully worked and oiled cutout holsters, his glance fixed on the south window.

"But four up-and-comin' gents is something else again!" he remarked.

Through that window could be seen a ribbon of rain-washed trail that joined with the slithering Lechuza a couple of miles distant. Along this trail, gigantic and distorted in the swirling mists, four men were swiftly riding in the direction of the ranch house.

As they drew nearer, Hatfield noted that one was a queer looking individual in a long black coat and a hard hat. Congress gaiters were thrust into box stirrups and he flopped about in the high Mexican saddle as if unaccustomed to horseback riding.

The other men wore broad-brimmed hats with high, dimpled crowns and were draped in black slickers, from which the rain streamed in glistening rivulets, and scuffed cowboy boots.

There were heavy curtains to the ranch house windows. Hatfield drew them close, shot the bolt on the outer door and waited. Soon he heard the soft chuck of the horses' hoofs on the soggy ground, then a popping of saddle leather and a jingling of bridle iron as the men dismounted. They clumped up the veranda steps, tried the locked door and knocked loudly, waited, and knocked a second time. There followed a low rumble of unintelligible words.

"Let's try 'round back," a voice suggested.

Hatfield listened to them clump down the steps. A moment later the kitchen door creaked open. Boots scuffed the floor.

"Good gosh amighty!" somebody squealed. "Take a look in here!"

A moment of tingling silence, then another man spoke, harshly, peremptorily:

"Scatter outa this, pronto. Stickney, you take the bunkhouse, Travis the stable. Crane, you and me'll go over the house. Shoot fust and ask questions afterward!"

Feet moved, then froze as from the darkened inner room a voice spoke, softly drawling, but pregnant with the menace of assured power.

"S'pose you stay put, gents, and *answer* some questions fust!"

CHAPTER 4
DANGER LIGHTS

Open-mouthed, the four men stood staring at the doorway of the inner room. A tall figure stood there, eyes glinting in the shadow of low-drawn hat brim and regarding them over the barrels of two long black guns.

Three pairs of hands shot into the air without question. But the fourth man, a lean individual with a stony face, who had unbuttoned his slicker, drew a gun with a flicker of movement too swift for the eye to follow.

Crash!

The drawn gun spun from the lean man's hand and slammed against the wall, its lock smashed by a heavy slug. Smoke wisped from one of Jim Hatfield's black muzzles. The Lone Wolf himself spoke again, his voice still lazily drawling, but edged with steel.

"Next one'll knock over something' 'sides

a hawglaig. You're fast, feller, but don't try it again if yore debts aren't all paid up. It'd be a shame to have yore creditors hafta look all over hell for you! Get 'em up higher!"

The other cursed venomously, but obeyed. The lanky individual in the hard hat spoke again, his voice quavering from a tight mouth that moved not at all:

"It's a serious matter to shoot a deputy sheriff, youngman! You can't trifle with the law like that."

Hatfield eyed the lean man with interest.

"Didn't shoot him — just plugged his gun," he remarked. "Mebbe that wouldn'ta happened if he hadn't spouted that 'shoot fust' of his. All right, Mistuh Dep'ty, and you other gents, face the wall, and keep elevated!"

Grumbling and mouthing, the four obeyed. Hatfield dexterously plucked guns from sheaths and laid them on the table beside the silent watchers who sat there. The man in the hard hat wore neither belt nor shoulder holster, but Hatfield removed a stubby, double-barreled derringer from either flapping sleeve.

"All set for a little sidewinder fangin', eh?" he remarked casually, but with hard eyes.

Placing the derringers on the table with the other hardware, Hatfield sat down, tilted his chair back against the wall, his high heels hooked over the bottom rung. He had holstered one gun, but the other lay idly in his lap, seemingly a very part of the slim, bronzed hand that held it.

"All right, turn around," he ordered.

Sullenly the four men obeyed. Hatfield focused his gaze on the lean man with the impassive face.

"Deputy sheriff, eh?" he questioned. "Got yore credentials with you?"

Silently the man brushed back his coat, showing a nickel badge pinned to his vest. Then he fumbled in an inner pocket, slowly and carefully, so that no gesture might be misunderstood by the grim figure in the chair, and brought forth several folded papers, which in obedience to Hatfield's gesture, he tossed into the Lone Wolf's lap.

Hatfield glanced at them, although his gaze apparently never left the men across the room. He refolded them and nodded.

"Reckon you're authentic, Cartwright," he admitted. "And these other gents?"

"I am Wilfred Crane, president of the Javelina Bank," the man in the hard hat broke in, "and I demand that you restore my — ah — property and cease menacing me with that weapon. You do otherwise at your peril."

Hatfield regarded him speculatively.

"*Javelina* — pig bank," he translated freely. "Where I was reared, we kept 'em in pens."

The two companions, who had cowhand written all over them, snickered loudly and even the stern-faced deputy grinned. But the smoothly shaven, bloodless countenance of the banker flushed darkly and he shot a black glare at the impassive Hatfield.

The deputy's face hardened again. "What'd you do with old Angus?" he asked.

Hatfield regarded him a moment.

"B'lieve I mentioned you were gonna *answer* a few questions," he remarked pointedly.

The deputy snorted through his nose, but Hatfield's momentary flash of humor had relieved the tenseness of the situation. For a moment he scrutinized the good-humored, careless faces of the two cowboys, then ran his gaze over the stern but not unpleasant countenance of the deputy. The banker he ignored. With swift, effortless ease he holstered the big gun.

"Reckon that shoot fust business is sorta in the discard," he remarked, "and I'm not worrying about anything else. When it comes my turn to answer questions, I figger I can do so to the satisfaction of all parties.

If you still feel oncertain about me, Dep'ty, I'll ride to town with you and talk to yore boss." Hatfield gestured toward the table.

"You gents can assemble yore hardware again whenever you're a mind to," he added.

The deputy nodded, but neither he nor the cowboys made any move to immediately retrieve their guns. Crane, the banker, took a half step but shuffled back again at an agate glance from Cartwright, the deputy sheriff.

The deputy rolled a cigarette and lighted it.

"Shoot," he nodded to Hatfield.

"Fust, which one is Travis and which is Stickney?" Hatfield asked, with a jerk of his thumb toward the cowboys.

"Fat feller hidin' behind the grin is Travis," the deputy introduced. "The little hungry lookin' jigger is Stickney." He glanced inquiringly at the Lone Wolf as the two punchers ducked their heads in acknowledgment.

"Hatfield," he supplied. "Jim is the front handle most folks use."

The scrawny little Stickney started at the name, shot his head forward, jerked it back, in which gesture he bore a ludicrous resemblance to a turkey gobbler.

"Feller," he spoke for the first time, "do

you happen to ride a golden sorrel hoss?"

"The sorrel horse is in the stable," Hatfield replied easily.

The others darted inquiring glances at Stickney, but the little cowboy did not choose to elaborate. He stared at Hatfield with something like awe in his gaze.

" 'Bout the feller you called Angus?" Hatfield addressed the deputy.

Wilfred Crane started to speak, but the deputy silenced him with a peremptory gesture.

"Angus McPherson owns this hacienda," the deputy explained. "Mr. Crane holds a note against the spread and a quarterly installment is due. He rode out to collect."

Hatfield stared at the deputy curiously. "I'm sorta new to this district," he remarked; "is it customary to send along a sheriff's posse to collect payment on a note?"

The deputy flushed slightly at the note of sarcasm in the Lone Wolf's drawling tones.

"Nope, it ain't usual," he admitted, "but ol' Angus is a salty gent and sorta quick-trigged to go on the prod. 'Pears him and Mr. Crane had words the last time they met. Mr. Crane come to the sheriff's office and int'mated he might need pertection. So Sheriff Mason told me to ride out with him to keep the peace if him and Angus got rambunctious. Bunty and Stick are sorta at loose ends right at present and they come along with me for the ride."

"Yep, nothing' else to do till we tie onto a job," corroborated Bunty Travis, Stickney nodding agreement.

"Protection?" Hatfield repeated, a trifle dryly. " 'Pears Mistuh Crane sorta packs his own protection," with a significant glance at the table.

"I am a law-abiding man," Crane protested with dignity.

Hatfield did not press the point. Instead, he gestured toward the four dead men. Cartwright and the others followed the movement of his hand with their eyes.

"Reckon you gents know what time it started raining last night?" he questioned.

All four nodded.

"Well," the Lone Wolf went on, "as I said before, my horse and rig are in the stable. Take a look at the rig and you'll see easy that I was in that rain quite a spell; was in it from the start, the fact is. And a look at the four gents sitting there will tell you right off that they weren't in it a-tall. Right?"

The deputy nodded shortly.

"Which goes to show," Hatfield continued, "that they got here 'fore the rain started.

Look 'em over, Cartwright, and you'll know for yoreself that they been dead a lot of hours. I figger they checked out 'fore the rain started. Which sorta counts me out as having anything to do with passing 'em on, doesn't it?"

Without replying, the deputy strode to the table and took hold of a dead arm. With a grunt he let it fall back stiffly.

"I'm goin' out to the stable," he announced, and left the room.

The two cowboys picked up their guns and holstered them. Wilfred Crane glanced hesitantly at Hatfield.

"Go 'haid," the Lone Wolf told him.

Crane slipped the deadly little short-guns back into their cleverly constructed sleeve pockets. A few minutes later the deputy returned.

"You win," he told Hatfield shortly, and with grudging admiration. "There shore ain't much them eyes of yores miss. You'd oughta be a peace officer. Only," he added dryly, "I don't figger to have ever seed a peace officer rig up a hoss to leave standin' jest like you did that daisy of a sorrel."

There was a twinkle in Hatfield's steady eyes, but he offered neither comment nor explanation.

"But where in blazes is Angus McPherson?" the deputy demanded.

"He shore wasn't here when I arrived, just about daybreak," Hatfield replied. "Didn't McPherson have no hands? There's nobody in the bunkhouse. Beds haven't been slept in of late, either."

"Angus let all his hands go a coupla weeks back," the deputy said. "Didn't have but four, all counted. It's a good spread, but a small one. I understand he was sorta short on ready cash and figgered to make out durin' the slack season with his Mexican cook and a wrangler. Got mad and fired the cook and wrangler three, four days back. Evidently hasn't hired anyone in their places yet. But where is he?"

Bunty Travis spoke up. "Why keep on fussin' 'bout Angus?" he asked querulously. "He'll show up. Off lookin' for a hand or two, mebbe, or on some business of his own."

"He'd better put in an appearance very shortly," Wilfred Crane remarked grimly. "If that payment isn't made within the prescribed limits, I will be forced to take legal action."

Cartwright was about to reply when somewhere outside the house sounded a faint shout.

"Bet that's Angus now!" exclaimed Bunty.

Hatfield crossed to the living room window and drew the curtain aside. Lumbering along the trail, vaguely seen through the swirling rain mists, was a big wagon drawn by four mules. Three figures occupied the wide seat. The body of the wagon was piled with trunks and bags.

"That's Greasy Pete, the teamster, from Javelina, and Snoot Montez, his helper, and — gosh, looks like a gal on the seat there with 'em!" Lance Cartwright spoke over Hatfield's shoulder.

"Shore is," agreed Stickney, "headed this way, too."

Hatfield acted swiftly. "Into the front room, ev'body," he ordered. "Shoot the bolt on that back door, Travis, and draw those kitchen curtains. Shove the curtains back in this room, and shut the kitchen door. Don't know what this is all about, but shore can't let a lady get a peek into that kitchen 'fore we move to make those four gents there comfortable. You open the front door and do the talking, Cartwright."

Up the trail rumbled the wagon, the big teamster whooping from time to time.

"Reckon Pete's got a snootful of red-eye aboard, per usual," remarked Travis.

Beside the veranda, Greasy Pete pulled up. He flipped the multiple reins about the whipstock with an expert gesture, leaped solidly to the muddy ground and, reaching up, swung the girl from the seat onto the porch with effortless ease. She hesitated, staring around with wide blue eyes, the water dripping from her flimsy raincoat and squishing from her soaked little shoes.

As Cartwright flung open the door she stepped forward, entered the room and stood glancing from one to another of the occupants. Her gaze focused on the elderly Crane.

"Are — are you my Uncle Angus?" she hesitated.

Her voice was soft and modulated but betraying a slight nervousness. She was little and slender, with deep blue eyes and hair the color of ripe corn.

"Reckon you mean Angus McPherson, ma'am," Cartwright's hearty voice replied. "Nope, that ain't him, ma'am. Angus is — is off on a little trip right now. You say he's yore uncle?"

The girl's nervousness appreciably increased. "Yes," she replied. "I — I have come to live with him. He wrote he would meet me at the stage station, but he did not."

"Reckon he just couldn't make it, ma'am," the deputy soothed, "but don't you worry.

36

He'll be right along, I'm shore. Best thing you can do now is trot upstairs to whatever room you pick out and change into some dry clothes. C'mon, boys, let's get the lady's trunks off the wagon and carry 'em upstairs."

They were moving toward the porch when the giant figure of Greasy Pete loomed in the doorway, with his shifty little helper slinking behind him.

Snoot Montez was a slithery sort of a little man, lithe and wiry. His enormous beak of a nose told whence came his nickname. He had astonishingly high cheekbones, a practically lipless mouth and eyes like little hot coals.

As he entered the room, those burning eyes in the inscrutable face fixed for a moment on Jim Hatfield. The tight lids dropped the merest fraction. Then his stare shifted to meet Wilfred Crane's eyes and Hatfield, who missed nothing, sensed that there was meaning of some sort in the swift exchange of glances. The faces of both men remained expressionless, however.

"A mighty nigh full blood Karankawa, or I'm a heap mistook," Hatfield told himself as the swarthy little man sidled along the wall in a self-effacing manner.

Hatfield fleetingly wondered how one of

the few surviving members of the ferocious tribe that once dwelt along the coast in the vicinity of Matagorda Bay came to be here in far west Texas. But his attention was quickly turned to Snoot's companion.

Greasy Pete swaggered into the room. "Jest a minute, gents," he rumbled, "the lady owes me a little bill for freightin'."

The girl flushed painfully. "I — I told you I have no money left," she faltered. "I told you my uncle would take care of the charges when we arrived at his place."

"Uh-huh," grunted Pete, "but he ain't here."

"I'm sure he will return shortly," the girl replied. "If you will just wait until —"

"Oh, I don't mind waitin' around — with *you!*" Greasy Pete replied with a leer that deepened the girl's color.

Before she could speak, Jim Hatfield stepped in front of her. He spoke, his voice softly drawling, but for the second time that day the deputy heard the steely note edging his quiet tones.

"You don't need to wait for yore uncle, ma'am," he said. "I been sorta usin' his premises today, and I figger I owe him a little bill for chuck and horse feed. I'll jest take charge of the bill for freighting yore trunks, and this gent wouldn't need to do

38

any waitin' around."

Greasy Pete swelled like an enormous frog. He glared at the Lone Wolf from his bloodshot little pig eyes and his face was gorged with blood.

"I ain't takin' no order from you, high-pockets," he rumbled, "I'm waitin' around as long as I please. You tend to yore own business!" He dropped a hairy paw to the big gun at his hip as he spoke.

"Poor Pete!" sighed little Stickney.

It seemed to the intent watchers that Jim Hatfield did not move at all. Pete yanked his gun from its sheath, and at the same instant slim fingers like rods of nickel steel closed on the teamster's corded wrist. There was a howl of agony from Pete and the gun clattered on the floor. He struck out blindly with his free hand, but before it had traveled six inches the blow was blocked and he was spun about as on a pivot.

Hatfield let go the wrist, gripped Pete by the back of the neck and the slack of his pants, lifted him from the floor as if he were a child, swung him forward and let go. There was a wild crashing of splintered wood and clang-jangling of shattered glass; then the sodden thud of the giant's body striking the wet earth a dozen feet below.

In what seemed like a continuation of that

terrific swing, the Lone Wolf's fist caught Snoot Montez on the side of the jaw. Snoot traveled six feet through the air and brought up in a far corner of the room, and stayed there. The knife with which he had lunged at Hatfield tinkled to the floor.

Jim picked it up, snapped the heavy blade in two with his slim fingers as if it were a rotten stick and flung the pieces out the door. Then, with easy grace, he turned to the trembling girl.

"Sorry, ma'am," he said, "but I reckon I done spoiled one of yore windows."

The girl shrank back from this terrible man of violence with the grim face and cold eyes. And then suddenly the Lone Wolf smiled down at her from his great height — a smile that flashed his even teeth startlingly white in his bronzed face, quirked the corners of his rather wide mouth and turned the cold eyes as warm and sunny as summer seas.

The girl ceased to tremble and under the laughing light of the darkly lashed green eyes she flushed rosily, but quite differently than she had under the regard of Greasy Pete.

"Thank you," was all she said. "I'll go upstairs now, if you don't mind."

As the two cowboys trudged out to get

the trunks off the wagon, Bunty Travis remarked in slightly awed tones:

"It's hard to tell who's got the most to worry about — a man that big jigger looks mean at, or a gal he smiles at! Gosh! Pete and Snoot ain't come to yet!"

CHAPTER 5
DEATH LISTENS IN

The trunks were upstairs by the time Pete and Snoot "came to." Pete started to curse with his first rational breath, but a bleak glance from Hatfield silenced him save for incoherent mutterings. Snoot Montez, his jaw swollen as if he were trying to swallow a lemon, glared balefully, but limped out without protest.

"That wagon'll come in handy," said Cartwright. "We plumb gotta get them bodies out of here 'fore the lil' lady comes down again. 'Sides, Don Beard, the coroner, will wanta look 'em over and see if he can figger out what cashed 'em in. I reckon it's all right to move 'em, ain't it?"

"We'll take a chance," Hatfield replied. "A coroner usually sits on the bodies where the death takes place, but this is sorta 'ceptional, I'd say, pertickler as there's no relatives or friends of the deceased 'round that anybody knows anything about. Let's load 'em up."

Working swiftly and efficiently, they loaded the bodies into the wagon bed and covered them with tarpaulins. Greasy Pete grumbled and snorted, but obeyed orders. Little Snoot's eyes were like burning coals as he mounted the seat beside Pete, but he had nothing to say.

"I'm not at all certain that this procedure is legal," Wilfred Crane complained querulously. "I do not wish to fall afoul of the authorities. After all, I have an interest in this property and feel that I should be consulted concerning what is done on it."

"I'm the authority hereabouts right now," the deputy growled, "and if anybody gets yanked on the carpet, it'll be me. You jest fork yore bronc and come on back to town. Ain't nothing you can do here till Angus shows up."

Hatfield turned to the cowboys. "Rec'lect you gents saying you were on the lookout for a job of riding," he remarked. "Well, looks to me like you've got a job right here. This spread will need hands, and the little lady hadn't oughta be left alone."

"But what about Angus?" Bunty Travis demurred. "Angus might not like it when he shows up."

"I don't figger Angus will offer any objec-

43

tions when, and *if* he shows up," Hatfield replied quietly.

Cartwright gave him a startled glance. "You figger somethin's happened to Angus?" he asked in low tones.

Hatfield glanced toward the wagon, where Pete was gathering up his reins and growling to Wilfred Crane, who had mounted his horse and pulled up alongside the front wheel.

"I'm not saying anything for shore, Cartwright," he replied in the same low tones, "but I'll tell you something I'm plumb certain about: five men sat down at that table in there some time last night; *four* stayed sitting."

"You mean that Angus —"

"I'm meaning nothing, yet," Hatfield interrupted. "But there's the marks of five glasses on the table, and the prints of five pairs of shoes in the dust under the table."

Cartwright stared at him in bewilderment.

"S'pose you amble out to the stable with me to get my horse," Hatfield suggested.

In the stable he did not immediately secure Goldy's rig. Instead, he led the deputy into one stall after another, pointing to the feed boxes of each in turn. After the fifth stall he paused.

"See?" he remarked. "Five horses 'sides

mine ate in this row of stalls last night. No horses here now. And it's about certain those four cashed-in gents didn't walk to get here."

Cartwright swore under his breath. "This is gettin' too damn complicated for me," he declared. "Let's be high-tailin' for town."

"Let's stop at the ranch house a minute," Hatfield replied.

They found the girl had changed and descended to the living room. She was talking with Bunty Travis, but turned her attention to Hatfield when the Lone Wolf entered.

"You're leaving?" she asked.

"Yes," Hatfield told her. "I'm riding to town now, but I'll be back a little later. The boys will look after ev'thing."

"I — I'm more grateful than I can tell you for all your kindness to a total stranger," she told him earnestly. "I really don't know how to thank you, Mr. —"

Hatfield supplied his name and introduced Cartwright.

"I'm Mary Zane," the girl told them. "Angus McPherson is my mother's brother. When she died, a few months ago, he wrote and invited me to come live with him. I have never seen him. I can't understand why he was not here to greet me."

45

"Don't you worry 'bout him, or anything, Miss Mary," Hatfield reassured her. "You just ask the boys here for anything you want done. They rode out to work for your uncle, now that the busy time is coming on."

He glanced meaningly at Stickney and Travis, who implied they understood with almost imperceptible nods.

The wagon was lurching out of sight through the mists as Hatfield and the deputy mounted and gathered up their reins. Wilfred Crane's flapping figure could be made out, hunched in his saddle, his bent back almost visibly oozing resentment.

"Ol' Moneybags don't take over-kind to interference of any sort in his affairs," Cartwright chuckled. "Oh, he's all right, I reckon, but he shore drives a tight bargain. Angus had better show up with that quarterly installment or Crane'll slip a foreclosure on his spread shore as shootin'. What in blazes we gonna do 'bout that li'l gal if Angus don't happen to show up?"

There was so much concern in the deputy's voice that Hatfield shot a swift glance in his direction. The worried look on Cartwright's craggy but not unattractive face pulled the corners of Hatfield's mouth up. He quickly decided that no matter what might have happened to her uncle, the "li'l gal" didn't have anything to worry about.

"How long a trip to town?" he questioned.

"Will take that darn wagon 'bout four hours," Cartwright replied. "A good hoss can make it in two. We turn almost due east a mile farther on. Nope, don't hit the Lechuza a-tall — take the east fork of this track. The Lechuza makes a business of *not* runnin' through towns!"

It was more than five hours, however, and the rainy day was drawing to a close when they pulled up before the sheriff's office with their grisly load. The fat and comfortable old sheriff listened to Hatfield's story with many grunts, and when it was finished he shot an inquiring glance at Cartwright. Hatfield saw at once that he relied on the judgment of the lean deputy.

"Reckon that's about the straight of it, Jeff," Cartwright nodded. "Shall we take the bodies over to Doc's place? Figger you'd better start inquiries about Angus and see if anybody knows where he went. Want me to take care of it?"

They deposited the bodies at the office of the white-whiskered coroner, whose comments were sulphurous.

"I'll p'form an autopsy and see what I can find out," he promised. "Looks like pizen of some sort to me. Mebbe the hellions jest

47

drank themselves to death, though. You know any of 'em, Lance? I never seed 'em before."

Hatfield found a stable for Goldy, and a little room over the stalls where he could spend the night. Then he and Cartwright dropped into an eating house nearby and "s'rounded a few helpin's" of chuck.

"Drop around to Doc's in the mawnin' for the inquest," Cartwright told him, and in reply to a casual question: "Telegraph office? Uh-huh, right around the next corner, in the same building' as the Overtrail Stage Station."

He glanced wonderingly at the Lone Wolf, but Hatfield vouchsafed no explanation.

A few minutes later Jim Hatfield entered the telegraph office. There he concocted a carefully worded message which he ordered sent to an address in Franklin, far to the southwest.

"I'll wait for the answer," he told the operator.

After a long time the reply came. The operator, sworn to silence by the rules of the company, glanced curiously at the Lone Wolf as he handed him the message, which was unsigned.

Coronado Mine in Vegas robbed three

days ago of nearly a hundred thousand dollars in gold ingots by parties unknown. Stage driver and two guards killed. No one left alive to identify robbers. Shipment supposed to be secret. Drift foreman named Coster missing from work. Heavy-set, dark hair shot with gray, blue eyes.

With a nod to the operator, Hatfield left the office. In the dark street outside he paused, the concentration furrow deep between his black brows.

"A hundred thousand in gold," he mused. "That's a lot of gold — better'n four hundred pounds. But four strong horses could handle it, all right, and riders. And," he added grimly, "*one* man would still need four horses, and one more to fork! And it 'pears that feller Angus McPherson was sorta pressed for ready cash!"

Suddenly he turned and stared into the darkness beside the building, darkness sliced by the golden bar of light streaming through the open window of the telegraph office. To his quick ears had come a sound as of stealthy, retreating footsteps. For a moment he stood tense and motionless, peering into the dark; but the sound was not repeated, and only the click of the telegraph sounder inside the room and the swish and patter of the rain without broke the silence.

But to the Lone Wolf, lonely rider of dim trails with deadly danger as a constant stirrup companion, and abnormally sensitive to impressions, it seemed that for the instant his cheek had been fanned by the icy breath of an unseen wing.

Chapter 6
Owlhoot Night

Hatfield decided to give the town of Javelina a once-over before going to bed. Very soon he decided it was quite a town. From scraps of conversation gathered at various saloons and *cantinas,* he learned that it was the center of a rich cattle and mining district.

Despite the rain, the main street was crowded with a jostling throng of cowboys in gay neckerchiefs and silken shirts of many hues. Miners in red or blue flannel shirts, corduroys and muddy boots. Dance hall girls with vivid lips and too-bright eyes. Gamblers in sober black relieved by the snowy white of their shirt fronts and the waxen pallor of their faces.

The bars, dance floors and gambling tables were busy, and getting busier as the night progressed. It was easy to see that it was pay day for the neighborhood spreads and for the mines back in the hills. Also, as Hatfield knew, the roundup season was at hand and there were many drifting punchers in town, hopeful of obtaining employment in the near future, and correspondingly reckless with what money they had left.

Several times Hatfield heard the crackle of six-shooters spatting through the tinkle of dance music and the bawl-bellerin' of what passed for song. Things were sure lively, and the Lone Wolf was thoroughly enjoying himself.

He paused in front of a big saloon near the head of the street. The wide window was brightly lighted and across the glass Hatfield read *Holloway's* in gold letters. Somehow the name struck a familiar chord and he stared at it with knitted brows. However, he was unable to place the association and with a shrug of his wide shoulders he entered the saloon.

The bar was packed three deep and there was scarcely room to move on the dance floor. Every table was occupied by intent players whose attention was wholly centered on their cards. Three roulette wheels spun merrily, the bouncing balls chuckling like cynical devils as they skipped from slot to slot to the accompaniment of cheerful profanity on the part of the gents who guessed wrong and chortles from those who had shown better judgment, for the moment.

Hatfield found a space at the far end of the bar, near the dance orchestra, and squeezed into it. A perspiring bartender poured him a drink and filled the glass a second time after the first one had vanished with surprising celerity. He grinned admiringly as Hatfield used that one for a chaser.

"One on the house," he invited, tipping the bottle. "Feller, you can take it!"

Hatfield took the third one slowly, watching the dancers, the gamblers and the constantly changing faces at the bar.

"The Lechuza Trail may skip this *pueblo* but just the same, a lotta gents what ride it know where to turn off, or I'm a heap mistook," he mused to himself as he noted certain tight-lipped groups with hard and watchful eyes who kept to themselves and missed little of what went on about them.

From time to time request numbers were called for from bar or dance floor, and always a graceful young Mexican with a pleasing voice responded.

"How about 'The Rimrock Trail,' *muchacho?*" somebody shouted.

With a bow and a smile, the Mexican looped the cord about his shoulders, ran slim, bronzed fingers over the strings with

53

the crisp touch of a master. The crowd at the bar, sensing a treat, hushed their chatter and stood expectant.

The Mexican threw back his black head, smiled at them with a flash of his white teeth and sang the stirring old cowboy song in a voice that was like the rush of silvery waters through golden sunlight, like the beat of the rain on the forest crown, like the wind that plays the harp of the leaves when the moonlight dies and the sky flames rose and scarlet with the dawn.

> Silver stars in the purple dark,
> And a dead man lyin' stiff and stark,
> Deaf to the wolf's lone wail;
> A drum of hoofs on the slope below,
> And that's death tailin' me, I know,
> As I ride the Rimrock Trail!

Men stood stiff and tense as the Mexican's voice pealed and thundered through the big room. The lights, the gleam of bottle and glass, the mahogany and the mirrors faded away and the beat of hoofs, the shimmer of starlight, the silent shape in the empty dark, the grim forms of pursuing vengeance and the white, haggard face of the fleeing killer were there.

With a crash of chords like the roaring

guns of a posse closing in, the music ended. For a moment there was silence, then a thunder of applause.

"Feller," complained the cowboy who had asked for a song, "the way you sing that makes a jigger start lookin' over his shoulder and walk faster. I'm scairt I ain't gonna sleep well tonight!"

There was a general laugh, which hushed abruptly as a voice rang out from across the room.

"That's him, Sheriff, that's the outlaw. Do your duty!"

CHAPTER 7
KILLER GUNS

As one man, the crowd turned toward the swinging outer doors. Sheriff Jeff Mason stood there, beside him Wilfred Crane, president of the Javelina Bank. It was Crane who had spoken.

Glances shifted back to Hatfield, who stood a little apart, regarding the pair in the doorway with cool, amused eyes. Under that steady look, the old sheriff shifted uncomfortably.

"Arrest him, I say," shouted Crane. "He is a menace to any community. Arrest him!"

The sheriff hemmed and hawed. "But what for, Wilfred?" he asked mildly.

"What for! Isn't he an outlaw?"

"I dunno," the sheriff admitted frankly. "*You* say he is, and I sorta rec'lect hearin' some yarns about a feller what looks like him, but you can't lock a feller up for that, although some of the yarns say he has been mixed up in quite a few killin's."

"Ever hear of him killing anybody who didn't have a killing coming?" Hatfield asked softly.

"That is beside the question," Wilfred Crane broke in. "No man has a right to take the law in his own hands. We have lawfully elected and appointed officers to enforce the law."

"Sometimes they sorta slip up, though," Hatfield commented.

There were several grunts of agreement from the neighborhood of the bar.

Crane was beginning an angry reply when the sheriff interrupted, addressing Hatfield.

"Jest the same, feller," he said, "I reckon you'd better be movin' on. We can do 'thout yore kind in this deestrict."

Hatfield smiled, with his lips; his eyes were coldly gray.

"Nope," he declined. "Not quite ready to move, yet. If you can get somebody to prefer charges against me, I'll submit to arrest, willingly. Otherwise, I'm staying on here a while. Rather 'spect to tie onto a job when I ride out to the McPherson spread tomorrow mawnin'."

The sheriff hesitated uncertainly.

"Charges!" exploded Wilfred Crane. "Didn't he shoot Deputy Cartwright?"

"Uh-huh, so you say," grunted the sheriff,

"but the danged contrary-minded coot won't prefer no charges, and you know it. What did he tell you when you spoke to him about that?"

Wilfred Crane looked as if he preferred not to remember what Lance Cartwright had told him.

"This is a law-abiding community, and I think he should be run out of it," he complained.

"Crane," said a voice from behind the pair, "I got a notion you're sorta right about that."

For an instant there was strained silence, then a voice exclaimed:

"Good gosh! It's Doc Holloway hisself!"

Hatfield had seen the speaker enter the room, and as the name was called, he placed his man. Doc Holloway! Gambler, ruthless killer. "The fastest man who ever packed a gun!" He recalled fabulous stories of the dissolute, icy killer who was said to bear a charmed life. No man living, it was said, had ever beaten Doc Holloway to the draw. No man, it was said, ever would.

And always, with the cunning of the damned, Holloway contrived to place the other man in the position of blame. There were rumors of outlawry, of killings that were nothing but plain murder; but nobody had ever been able to prove anything against Holloway. He had been a member, it was said, of the old Tombstone, Arizona, gang of killers and highwaymen, one with Curly Bill Brocas, John Ringo and the Clantons. He was also said to have consorted with the notorious Kingfisher.

He moved from place to place, always well supplied with money, always respectably in business of some sort or other, usually saloon or gambling hall. He claimed to be an exponent of law and order and often had the authorities on his side in controversial matters.

All this flashed through Jim Hatfield's mind as he stared at the tall, amazingly thin figure of the man who stood regarding him from dead eyes in the face of a corpse. Cadaverous, bloodless, with gaunt features that did not move a muscle, Holloway looked like something that was newly risen from the grave. He was said to be consumptive, to know that early death was his inevitable portion, and perhaps from that knowledge came the recklessness that made his name a byword for fearlessness in the Southwest.

His hands were long, deathly white, with smooth tapering fingers not unlike those of Wilfred Crane. They looked like poised spearheads as they hung limply at his sides, close to the heavy, pearl-handled guns that jutted out from his swung-back black coat.

"Fast!" Hatfield told himself. "Lightning fast! No nerves a-tall. Accurate as he is fast."

His swift, all-seeing glance noted the solid planting of Holloway's feet, the rigid erectness of his long body.

"But he's got a weak spot!" the Lone Wolf exulted.

Lounging easily, the amused smile still quirking his lips, he gave Holloway back stare for stare.

"You a sheriff, too?" he asked mildly.

The sarcastic question seemed to slightly shake Holloway's icy reserve. For the first time, Hatfield saw him blink. But when he spoke, his voice was coldly unemotional, as before.

"I am not," he replied, "but I am a law-abiding citizen of this community."

"That makes two, and both admit it," Hatfield interrupted. "Gosh, this community is outfitted prime."

Holloway was opening his mouth to speak, when Hatfield suddenly blazed at him in a voice that resounded through the room.

"Stop it! Stop yore damn build-up! Stop it and get goin'. I know what you're here for, and I know what you're buildin' up to!

This time, Holloway, it won't work. This time you're gonna get told off and told off proper. You're here for a killin', if you can get away with it. You're nothing but a cold-blooded, murdering, hydrophobia skunk. You're a sidewinder, a desert crawler, ready to fang in the dark and then slide outa sight. Yore hand's called! Play yore cards or throw 'em into the discard!"

There was a concerted gasp of amazement that ran over the room like a prairie fire. Men stared in unbelief. Doc Holloway "called!" Taunted! Dared to draw! It was suicide!

Eyes blazing, lips drawn back, his tall form rigid as poised steel, Jim Hatfield faced the corpse-featured killer. He saw Holloway's shoulder muscles swell, saw murder flare in his dead eyes.

Then Holloway drew!

The eyes told Hatfield he was going to draw, and Hatfield knew he could never hope to beat, even to match, that blinding speed that was not human.

He didn't even try. As Holloway's hand flickered like the shadow of death's wing, the Lone Wolf hurled himself sideways and down. His body had not struck the floor before death was hissing and screaming through the space it had occupied the split second before.

Jim Hatfield's hair-trigger mind had read aright the killer's weakness. Solidly planted on his widespread feet, Holloway shot where his eyes were focused. And before he could shift his aim, long lances of flame gushed from Hatfield's right hand.

They seemed to center on Holloway's breast, those lancing spurts of flame, and at their touch, the killer reeled back as from a mighty blow. A choking cry burst from his lips, his eyes stared wildly, unbelievingly. He tried to shift the pearl-handled gun, but it dropped from his nerveless fingers and thudded sullenly on the floor.

And with a crash, Doc Holloway's tall figure fell across it!

CHAPTER 8
STEALTHY MURDER

In a single supple movement Hatfield was on his feet. He had a gun in either hand now, his gray eyes glinted over the room, and the black muzzles of those guns, one still wisping smoke, seemed to single out every man there for special and individual attention.

Dance floor girls were screaming, chairs were pushing back from the tables. Men stared with awestruck eyes at the man who had downed the most notorious killer Texas had ever known. For a long moment, nobody made a move, nobody spoke. They just stood and stared. And then pandemonium broke loose and through it knifed Wilfred Crane's vindictive yell:

"Now will you act, Sheriff Mason? He's just murdered a prominent citizen in cold blood!"

Before the sheriff could reply, a harsh voice rang out:

"Murder, nothin'! That was self-defense or I never seed it! Doc drawed fust and shot fust. He jest missed, that was all. If this feller hadn't shot back, Doc woulda drilled him dead center 'fore he coulda got off the floor. Doc asked for it, and got it, and he had it comin'!"

There was a chorus of agreement. At the same instant a tall figure pushed through the swinging doors. It was Lance Cartwright, the deputy sheriff.

"You're right!" exploded Cartwright. "I saw it all through the window. Jeff, you better take Mistuh Crane outa here 'fore he strains a ligament or somethin'!"

After Sheriff Jeff Mason and the banker had departed, Crane still mouthing complaints, Hatfield and Cartwright left the saloon together.

"Feller," said the deputy, "I don't know what this is all about, but that was as plain a case of attempted premeditated murder as I ever seed, and I still don't know how he didn't come to get away with it. How did you do it?"

"Holloway had a weakness," Hatfield replied. "He was fast — fastest man I ever saw or ever 'spect to see — but he hadda get set. He made up his mind where he was gonna shoot and shot there. He couldn't shift his aim fast. He calc'lated the other feller would allus try to beat his draw, and he knew the other feller couldn't, that's all. I jest figgered it out and acted accordingly to throw Holloway off balance. Nothing to it."

"Uh-huh," Cartwright agreed dryly. "I see — somethin' like pokin' your finger in a rattlesnake's eye and then outsmartin' *him!* Uh-huh, plumb simple! But why in blazes did Holloway want to cash you in?" he demanded. "You ever have a run-in with him afore?"

Hatfield smiled down at him and made a reply that left Cartwright still more at a loss.

"Gamblers usually hang together," Hatfield said.

From the tone of Hatfield's voice, Cartwright knew that further questioning would be futile. With an exasperated grunt, he changed the subject.

"Here's Doc Beard's office," the deputy said, indicating a lighted window with a jerk of his thumb. "S'pose we drop in and see what he found out about them four gents we delivered."

They found the old doctor at his desk. He grunted and snorted at Cartwright's question.

"Pizen of some sort," he declared, "that's

as much as I can make out. Nothin' I know or ever heard tell of. Injun pizen, most likely. 'Pears to be some sort of an alkaloid, sorta like a form of mushroom pizening, I'd say, such as the *Deadly Amanita,* but not jest the same."

Hatfield gave the old doctor a keen glance. "I sorta had a notion that kinda poison brought on convulsions, violent ones," he remarked.

Doc Beard nodded. "That's so," he admitted, "and it shore has me puzzled. Lance here tells me those four jiggers were sittin' peaceful 'round a table, like they'd jest nacherly got tired of livin' and decided to give themselves up. Folks sufferin' convulsions or violent vomitin' don't die that way. Well, mebbe Angus McPherson can throw some light on the subject when he shows up."

"If he ever shows up!" Cartwright grunted.

"What you mean by that, Lance?" asked Beard.

"Well," Cartwright replied slowly, "Hatfield here showed me purty conclusive that there was five men settin' round that table drinkin. Four of 'em stayed there; one got up and went away. Now who would that one have been? Angus McPherson had let all his hands go and there wasn't nobody left at the ranch house but him. Who but Angus woulda been there late in the evenin', when those four fellers evidently arrived. If Angus was the fifth feller at that table, you wouldn't hardly 'spect him to show up round hereabouts again, would you?"

"But why in the blankety-blank-blank would ol' Angus wanta pizen four hellions he never seed afore?" demanded Doc Beard.

Cartwright shrugged. "*Mebbe* he never seed them afore," he countered. "Then mebbe he did. We don't know everythin' about Angus McPherson. He ain't been here over-long. I rec'lect, he come here and bought the Bar M jest a year or so 'fore Wilfred Crane showed up and took over the bank, and Crane's been here less'n two years. Angus mighta had good reasons for doin' in them four gents. If not Angus, who else?"

Doc Beard could not answer that question and profanely admitted it. Instead he called to an urchin who was dangling his legs from a chair in the outer office.

"Come here, son, here's Wilfred Crane's sleepin' powders you can take over to him.

"You speakin' about Crane made me rec'lect the boy was waitin'," he told Cartwright. "I'd jest finished makin' up the perscription when you come in. Crane takes enough of that stuff every right to put a boss to sleep. If he wasn't allus cudgelin' his brains how to make an extra dollar, mebbe he'd sleep better o' nights."

"He's a cantankerous coot, all right," admitted Cartwright, "and when he's down on a feller, he's shore down on him for keeps. But he's allus plumb square in his dealin's, even though he is almighty close at a bargain. And he shore put the Javelina Bank back on its legs. She was mighty tottery when Crane took over from ol' John Purdy. Reckon John was a mite easy-goin'."

"Ain't nothin' easy-goin' about Wilfred Crane!" grunted old Doc.

"I know it," replied Cartwright with a worried air. "I'm almighty scairt he'll be foreclosin' on the Bar M if that payment ain't made pronto. There's plenty of steers on the Bar M to take care of it, too, or I'm a heap mistook. But gettin' 'em combed outa the brakes and rounded up for market in time is a mite of a chore. Bunty Travis and Stick are good hands when they got somebody to tell 'em proper what to do, but they ain't no great shakes at thinkin' for themselves. Goin' to bed, Hatfield?"

"Uh-huh," the Lone Wolf replied, rising and stretching his long arms above his head.

"Gotta be up early. I've a notion there's a foreman's job sorta waitin' out to the Bar M Spread!"

CHAPTER 9
GOLD IS WHERE YOU FIND IT

The double inquest was held with cow country speed and efficiency, and with scant regard for legal formalities. The coroner's jury, after hearing the testimony of Hatfield, Cartwright and Doc Beard, 'lowed that the four unknowns met death at the hands of party or parties unknown, and recommended that the sheriff take steps to learn the dead men's identities, if possible, and to run down Angus McPherson and learn what he had to say.

Doc Holloway, it was opined, jest nacherly tried it once too often and woulda cashed in purty soon from consumption, anyhow.

Mid-morning saw Jim Hatfield riding for the McPherson ranch, the Bar M. He whistled gayly as he rode through the golden sunshine, for the rain had ceased during the night.

He found Bunty Travis and Tate Stickney

puttering about the ranch buildings and obviously awaiting somebody to give orders. They got them, in a hurry.

"Gotta get a trail herd together for shipment, pronto," Hatfield said, "else that lantern-jawed banker will drop his loop on the spread. Can't wait for Angus McPherson to show up. The little lady is boss while he's away and I reckon she'll string along with what I suggest. Lance Cartwright is sendin' out an ol' Mexican woman to do the cooking and look after the house. The wagon will bring yore warbags you asked for, too."

They went to work on the trail herd with a will. There were plenty of good cattle on the spread, but they were badly scattered and with the natural contrariness of beef critters, sought out the most inaccessible brakes and canyons to hole up in.

But Travis and Stickney were skilled hands and cheerful workers. All they needed was somebody to tell them what to do, and Hatfield told them. He himself worked harder than either, and at the same time he was constantly examining every inch of the terrain they covered, looking for the signs and clues he felt confident were to be found.

"Couldn't have moved that four hundred pounds of bar gold very far, or I'm a heap mistook," he told Goldy. "It's holed up somewhere on the spread, waiting for a chance to be snuk out. Fust good and stormy night that happens along, I figger. And if I can't get a line on where it is 'fore then, it's liable to make a clean getaway, and that's a sight too much money to let trail its rope."

Three busy days passed before Hatfield got to town again. He dropped in at the sheriff's office and found Lance Cartwright at the sheriff's desk. Cartwright's greeting was cordial, but his face was grave. Opening the desk drawer, he drew forth a circular such as are sent out by sheriffs' offices of various counties.

"Come in from Presidio County, down in the Big Bend country," Cartwright said.

Hatfield took the circular and gazed at the scowling, hard-eyed face depicted. Below the likeness he read:

WANTED
FOR QUESTIONING

Ralph Coster, lately employed as drift foreman at Coronado Mines, Vegas. Unaccountably missing from job and habitation. Suspected of complicity in robbery of Coronado Mine gold shipment valued at one hundred thousand dollars, in commission of which stage driver and two guards were murdered.

A description of the wanted man followed. Hatfield glanced up to meet Cartwright's gaze.

"It's him, all right," declared the deputy, "the short, husky one with the gray hair, the one what wore the laced boots. One hundred thousand in gold! Whe-e-ew! Feller, that's a pocket fulla *dinero!*"

"The Coronado Company evidently thinks so," Hatfield remarked. "See they're offering five thousand dollars reward for its return, and another thousand for the capture and conviction of the robbers. And *that* is folding money, too!"

Cartwright nodded emphatically. "And them four jiggers was the ones that pulled that job, shore as you're a foot high! But where's the gold?"

"That's yore question, feller," Hatfield grinned. "Smart, weren't they? Didn't head for Mexico, as everybody would figger them to do. Took the long chance and hit the Lechuza Trail for the nawth. Figgered if they could jest get a head start, they'd be okay.

"The Lechuza doesn't run through any towns, and while the posses were busy combing the country to the south and west, they'd be hightailin' for New Mexico and the mountain country where they'd be safe. But it appears they ran into a mite of bad luck."

"And it appears ol' Angus McPherson had a mite of *good* luck, of its kind!" Cartwright added bitterly. "Nope, I don't figger anybody hereabouts will get a chance to ask Angus any questions."

Hatfield nodded agreement. "Don't figger they will," he said.

"But Wilfred Crane and that donkey-haided boss of mine is askin' 'em, and supplyin' answers," Cartwright went on disgustedly. "Crane is intimatin' the gold was right there at the Bar M ranch house when you rode in, and that mebbe Angus was there, too, and had sorta disappeared when me and the boys and Crane arrived."

"Meaning that I did away with McPherson, and the gold, too," Hatfield remarked quietly.

" 'Bout the size of it," Cartwright replied. "Didja ever hear sich damphoolishness! Makes me wanta laugh."

"Usually isn't much to laugh about in a situation like that," Hatfield said gravely, "pertickler when a feller sorta has a reputation already."

Cartwright's face twisted into a frown, but Hatfield spoke again before he could comment.

"May need you in a hurry soon, feller," he said. "If I send for you, don't ask questions but come a-hightailin'. Okay?"

Cartwright held out a sinewy hand. "Okay!" was all he said.

Hatfield left the sheriff's office in a decidedly pleasant frame of mind.

Hatfield and Bunty Travis worked the north range of the Bar M the following day. It was the range nearest the ranch house, but also the toughest. The eastward curve of the Guadalupes was close and the hills were broken and craggy. Box canyons, dry washes, narrow ravines and scrambled ridges were jumbled together; but fat steers hid in the watered canyons and fed on the flowering weeds that clothed the sides of the washes.

Hatfield and Bunty spent a busy day and turned home late in the evening with a bunch that justified their efforts. Suddenly the fat cowpuncher rose in his stirrups.

"Look," he said, pointing with a plump forefinger. "Over there by the scrub oak. There's a hoss and he looks to be in bad shape."

They turned their mounts, and the tired

cattle took advantage of the respite to grab a few mouthfuls of succulent grass.

The horse was in bad shape, hardly able to move because of deep sores a hand-breadth in width just back of his withers.

"Saddle galls," grunted Travis, "but good gosh! what a load the pore devil musta been carryin' to git that way. Saddle bags musta been packed with lead!"

"I got some ointment in my pouch," Hatfield remarked, a peculiar light in his green eyes. "We'll give this pore feller a little doctorin'."

As Hatfield was procuring the ointment, Bunty gave an exclamation. He was staring at the brand on the lame horse's haunch.

" 'Cross-in-a-Box,' " he read. "Now where in blazes did this cayuse come from? There ain't no Cross-in-a-Box spread anywheres in this district."

"I rec'lect seeing that brand way down in the lower Big Bend country once," Hatfield remarked.

"Feller, you're a long ways from home," Bunty told the horse as they applied the soothing ointment to the sores. "Reckon some hellion what had oughta have his laig slit rode you up here and then set you loose when you got sore. I hope that hyderphobia skunk has sores like these to sit on!"

Hatfield nodded agreement to the fat cowboy's indignation, which he shared, with reservations. As he did everything possible to make the mistreated animal comfortable, his keen eyes were studying the locality and impressing landmarks indelibly on the tablets of his mind.

"Couldn't have come far, the shape he's in," he muttered as Bunty went to get his horse. "Bronc this sore wouldn't hardly move from where he was turned loose. And that's where a jigger who doesn't know over much about horses slipped bad!"

The north range was properly worked out when Hatfield and Bunty left it that evening, but just the same, mid-morning found the Lone Wolf back in the locality where they had encountered the stricken horse.

The Cross-in-a-Box cayuse was still there, quite near where they had left him beside a trickle of water, but he was visibly improved. Hatfield gave him another dose of ointment and then began a careful examination of the ground.

"Critter wouldn't have crossed the crick in his shape," he reasoned; "so he musta been turned loose on this side. He'd make for water, the closest he could find, and he'd try to travel down hill. Which sorta figgers he musta come outa one of those canyons

77

or washes to the nawthwest. Question is, which one? If it hadn't rained so hard and so long, there might be some tracks. As it is, I reckon I'll just nacherly hafta quarter the section."

Hour after hour Hatfield combed the canyon and wash, passing by those which contained water, for he felt confident the sore horse would not have strayed from convenient water and grass. The sun was approaching the zenith when he noted the first encouraging sign. Where a heavy cluster of overhanging branches had somewhat turned the rainfall was a deeply scored hoof mark, a mark that pointed *up* canyon. Hatfield studied it with care.

"Horse that made that print was carrying a heavy load," he interpreted the mark. "May have been the sore-backed critter, or one of the other three that I haven't seen hide or hair of all afternoon. Of course the others may have been in good shape to travel and were run off somewhere. Chances are they were. Anyhow, this crack in the hillside will stand a little once-over."

It was really little more than a crack, a narrow box canyon that grew even narrower as it bored into the hills. Hatfield rode slowly, scanning every inch of the ground with eyes that missed nothing. A second deeply scored print at the base of an over-hanging rock brought an exultant exclamation to his lips. Then the canyon petered out to a narrow slit that ended against a lofty wall with equally tall and perpendicular walls on either hands.

Shaking his head with disappointment, Hatfield turned back. But now he gave his entire attention to the side walls of the canyon and the thick straggle of growth that bristled up from the base of the cliffs. He was halfway down the canyon when the appearance of a clump of brush caught his eyes.

It was an evergreen growth, but the shiny leaves had a dull and grayish tint different from those which flanked this particular bush on either side. Hatfield turned Goldy and rode close.

"Look, feller!" he exclaimed. "Those leaves are wilted, and they hadn't oughta be."

He dismounted, wormed his way under the bush and found that the stout trunk, instead of being naturally rooted in the ground, was thrust into a crevice between two stones. The bush had been cut, and transferred to this spot from some other place.

Hatfield started to haul it from its artificial

stand, then abruptly changed his mind. Instead, he carefully worked his way under and around the prickly bristle, wincing at the bite of the thorns, but refraining from breaking branch or twig. Finally he made it, at the expense of a little skin, and stood staring at a dark opening in the face of the cliff. He crept closer and peered within. It was the mouth of a cave extending an unguessable distance into the canyon wall.

Hatfield considered a moment, then turned and pushed his way along the face of the cliff. In a shallow dry wash he found an abundance of dried sotol stalks which would make excellent torches. Securing several, he returned to the cave mouth. There he lighted one and entered the narrow passage.

There was barely room for him to stand erect at first, but after a few feet the roof lifted and the walls fell back. Another moment and he was in a wide, earth-floored cavern whose extent he could not estimate. He was but a few yards from one wall, the light of the torch disclosed, but the other was shrouded in darkness. He took a few steps in its direction and halted abruptly.

"Gosh!" he exclaimed, "lucky I didn't come groping round here in the dark!"

He was standing on the very lip of a

chasm that sank into dark and unknown depths. He turned and retraced his steps toward the near wall, holding his torch high. The wall was irregular, with juts of stone and shallow recesses. Before one of these recesses he paused, peering at the unmistakable evidence of freshly turned earth.

Hatfield fingered his heavy knife, but decided it was hardly suitable for digging. It was not far to the mouth of the cave, however, and he hurried out, found a stout trunk with a number of branches forking out in a cluster. He hacked the bush off close to the ground and cut and trimmed the branches until he had what could pass for a spade. With this he returned to the cave and went to work.

Removing the earth, which had been packed and stamped, was a tough job with his makeshift implement, but Hatfield persisted until he struck a tough but yielding obstacle. Another half hour and he had uncovered a stout leather saddle bag which taxed his strength to drag from the hole. It clanked dully as he drew it forth. Undoing the buckled flap, Hatfield peered within. The torch light reflected a yellowish gleam.

"Ingots," he muttered, "gold ingots; reckon this is the cache, all right."

Prodding with the "spade" met with the

same yielding resistance, which convinced Hatfield that other saddlebags containing ingots lay in the shallow hole. Then with a grim face he turned to another spot which bore the signs of recent excavation — a long, narrow rectangle, in this instance. Here he dug with the greatest care, shoveling the loose earth away with his hands.

Finally he stared into a marred and distorted face crowned by a thatch of grizzled hair. A little more digging uncovered a gray flannel shirt blotched with dark and ominous stains.

"Knifed in the back, 'tween the shoulder blades," Hatfield deduced. "Jigger was an expert with the sticker, too. Figger he hit the heart first try. Poor ol' feller, you never had a chance!"

Face bleak, eyes cold as wind-swept ice, he stared down at the pitiful remains for a moment. Then he reverently replaced the disturbed earth. He likewise covered the bag of gold, patting and smoothing the spot until a casual glance would fail to note evidence of an intruder.

"Just in case there might be a slip-up," he muttered as he headed for his horse.

CHAPTER 10
LEAD AND STEEL

Heavy clouds were banking up in the west and the low-lying sun was sullenly red as the Lone Wolf rode swiftly toward the Bar M ranch house. He scanned the ominous sky with satisfaction as he noted a flicker of distant lightning and a cold breath fanned his cheek.

"Storm coming shore as shooting," he told Goldy, "and at this time of the year when they do come in this section they're usually sockdollagers. This will be the kinda night those hellions have been waiting for, or I'm a heap mistook.

"It'll be made to order for them, 'cording to their way of thinking, and they won't take the chance of waiting for another. Rain storms aren't so frequent hereabouts, and I've a notion they're getting itchy fingers."

Hatfield pulled up at the bunkhouse as the sun vanished behind the grim spires of the Guadalupes. Ten minutes later little Tate

Stickney was riding with all speed to Javelina.

Hatfield ate his supper and then made a few preparations. He wrapped a bundle of oil-soaked waste into a poncho and strapped it behind his saddle. Goldy had put away a sizable helping of chuck and enjoyed a good rubdown. He seemed fit for anything when Hatfield rode away through the rain that began to fall shortly after dark.

The wind was rising and there were mutters of thunder in the west. Hatfield paused where the trail forked toward Javelina and he and Goldy sought what shelter they could find beneath a tree. A half hour passed before the Lone Wolf heard the beat of swiftly approaching hoofs.

"Hope Tate made the grade," he muttered, straining his ears.

As they approached the fork in the trail, the hoofbeats slackened to a walk. A low whistle sounded through the rain-streaked dark. Hatfield whistled a reply and a moment later Tate Stickney and Lance Cartwright loomed before him.

"Thanks, feller," Hatfield said to the deputy. "You come through pronto."

"When I say I'll string along with a jigger, I mean it," Cartwright replied simply.

Stickney turned off at the bunkhouse, but

Hatfield and the deputy rode northward through the rain. With unerring instinct, the Lone Wolf sought out the mouth of the cave.

"I marked a spot a few hundred yards further up canyon where we can leave the broncs under a big overhang," Hatfield told Cartwright. "They'll be outa the wet there."

They made the horses comfortable and then stole back through the brush to the cave mouth. In a niche just beyond the grave and the cache they took their stand.

Slowly the hours passed, and Hatfield began to wonder if his hunch about the first rainy night might be in error. It was well past midnight when there was a sound in the direction of the cave mouth. Voices speaking in conversational tones reached them.

"Don't suspect a thing," Hatfield whispered to the deputy. "Think they're riding a clear trail. All set, pardner?"

Cartwright grunted an affirmative and crouched low.

A light winked down the passage, drew steadily nearer. By the blaze of a torch, Hatfield could see two figures approaching. He stepped out of the niche, breathed a word to Cartwright. There was the scratch of a match, then a roaring flame shooting to the roof as the oiled waste caught fire. The whole scene was light as day.

Bathed in the radiance, dazzled by the unexpected glare, the approaching figures halted in mid-stride. Slightly in advance was the stringy form of Snoot Montez. Behind him was tall, gaunt Wilfred Crane in his flapping black coat.

Like the blare of a bugle Jim Hatfield's voice rang out:

"Trail's end for you and the Karankawa, Crane. Elevate!"

"In the name of the State of Texas!" Cartwright's voice echoed the command.

As if jerked by strings, Wilfred Crane's long arms shot above his head, "reachin' for the sky!"

But the banker's supple wrists snapped downward like darting spear points. The stubby derringers in his sleeves smacked against his palms, their blunt muzzles spouting flame. It was the "gambler's draw," bewilderingly unexpected, before which many a fast gunman had died.

But even as Crane pulled trigger, his body slewed sideways as if hurled by a mighty hand. The bullets from his short forty-ones screeched wildly through the darkness and Wilfred Crane slumped forward onto his face.

Hatfield's guns flamed again, and the vicious little Karankawa's knife hissed past Cartwright's head. Snoot Montez himself leaped into the air with clutching hands, as if seeking to grasp his own departing soul, and fell beside the writhing banker.

Cartwright ran forward. "Snoot's done for," he shouted, kneeling beside the pair. "But Crane —"

"Look out!" roared Hatfield, hard on his heels.

Out of the dark passage leaped a gigantic figure. Cartwright was struck down across the dead Montez. Hatfield ducked under Greasy Pete Hawes' clubbed gun and closed with the giant. He had no chance to use the gun he still held in his own right hand and dropped it as he clutched at Pete's corded wrist.

A wrench and a twist and Pete dropped his own gun with a howl of pain. But at the same instant his great fingers closed on the Lone Wolf's throat. Breast to breast, straining, heaving, gasping for breath, the two men struggled.

The giant was as tall as Jim Hatfield, and full seventy pounds heavier. His strength was enormous and he was mad with rage. Hatfield slashed and cut his face with wicked short-arm blows, but Pete only blew bloody bubbles, grunted and tightened his terrible grip on the Lone Wolf's throat.

A band of hot iron seemed to encircle Hatfield's laboring breast, his temples throbbed and pounded, a rosy, oval-tinted mist swam before his eyes. His lungs were bursting for air and the blood roared in his veins. He heard the giant grunt with triumph, felt the sweaty wrist slip in his slackening grasp.

And then with one final prodigious effort he hurled himself backward to the ground. His left hand darted out and seized Pete's other wrist at the same instant, and as the giant's great form hurtled over him, his right leg, rigid as a bar of steel, drove upward.

Caught in the terrific leverage of that upward driving foot and the downward pull on his wrists, Greasy Pete seemed to have taken unto himself wings. His huge body soared upward and, as Hatfield let go his wrists, turned a complete somersault in the air, described an arc and shot downward. It cleared the lip of the chasm and with an awful shriek of terror and despair, vanished in the black dark.

Dizzy and gasping, Hatfield got to his feet. He gulped great breaths of life-giving air, felt of his bruised throat and shook his black head to free it of shadows. His strength came back quickly, his head cleared and he knelt beside the deputy. Cartwright was already groaning with returning consciousness and in a moment sat up, rubbing his sore head.

"This new hat saved me a busted skull," he mumbled. "She's thick and stiff."

Hatfield stepped into the deep shadows to examine the body of Wilfred Crane, and muttered bitterly. There was nothing there. Crane was missing!

"What's the matter?" demanded Cartwright as he got weakly to his feet.

"Crane!" said Hatfield tersely. "He got away. He must have dropped just an instant before I fired at him."

"He'll never dare show his face in this part of the country again," said the deputy. "Not now, when he is certain that we know as much as we do about him."

Jim Hatfield swung around toward the passage, as though to go in search of the banker, and then stopped. He knew that any hope of finding Crane in the darkness was futile. Yet he would never give up the chase until the man was caught.

"We know it was Wilfred Crane that has been back of all the trouble around here," said Cartwright. "But why?"

"Too much gold," said Hatfield. "Crane

couldn't resist it. He either saw what those four hellions were packing or they told him about it. He knew one or more of them — the gambler, I'd say — gamblers seem always to know each other, and stick together, like Crane and Holloway, for instance."

"But what was Crane doin' at the ranch house that night, and where was Angus McPherson?" asked Cartwright.

"Crane rode to the Bar M to see about the money Angus owed him," Hatfield explained. "Angus wasn't there, and Crane made himself at home and waited. He was there when those four fellers rode up. Angus didn't get there until the killing was over, the chances are. Snoot Montez, who was with Crane and had been his man in Crane's gambling days, killed Angus while the old man was putting his horse in the stable."

Deliberately Jim Hatfield blew out the flaming torches and stamped on the smoldering waste. The ranger had not forgotten that Crane had escaped and might try to ambush the men who had spoiled his plans.

There was something hard beneath Hatfield's right foot as he moved around. He reached down and picked it up. It was one of the derringers that Crane had carried in his sleeves. Hatfield found the other small gun nearby. That meant the banker was unarmed and doubtless had not lingered in the vicinity.

"How do you know it was Montez that killed Angus?" asked the deputy, his voice coming eerily out of the darkness.

"By the feed boxes in the stalls," answered Hatfield. "Recollect I showed you five recently used feed boxes on one side of the stable? I didn't show you the two on the other side. One where Snoot's hoss ate, and one with feed in it that hadn't been touched. I knew there had been six men in that kitchen, and that shore puzzled me for a while, as only five men drank at the table. Montez didn't drink with the others."

"Why?"

"Because he wouldn't have been able to take it."

"The poison?" asked the deputy.

"Nope, not the poison. That was the point that had me fooled for a while. To say that one man can slip poison into the glasses of four men and keep his own clean at the same time is *loco* talk. It can't be done. But to slip somethin' into the jug everybody is drinkin' from is easy, and that's just what Crane did."

"Then why didn't it kill Crane, too?"

"Tell you the rest after we get ridin'," said Hatfield. "Let's go."

Hatfield and Cartwright rode slowly homeward under a clearing sky after searching for some time in the vague hope of finding further trace of the banker. The deputy was still curious.

"Why didn't the poison kill Crane?" he asked.

"Because when Crane was drinkin' with the other four, there wasn't any poison in the jug."

"You got my rope tangled like a rattler in a cactus patch," snorted Cartwright. "Tie hard and fast, feller, so's I can see which way the twine stretches."

"Remember the night we talked with Doc Beard, in his office? Well, Doc was just sendin' Wilfred Crane a box of sleeping powders, and Doc remarked that Crane took enough every night to put a hoss to sleep? That was where I struck pay dirt. What Crane did was to slip a whopping dose of his sleeping powder into the jug. He knew he could stand up under what would knock the other jiggers cold.

"When they began to pass out, he slipped in the poison and of course didn't take the last drink with them. They were too sleepy to notice that he didn't. That's why Montez didn't drink at the table with the others. The sleeping powder would have knocked him out, too. And of course the powder explains why they didn't have convulsions from the poison."

Hatfield paused to roll a cigarette, then went on.

"I'm tellin' you all this so you can sort of explain things to the folks around here," he said. "I figger on trailin' after Crane, so I won't be around much longer."

"Good!" exclaimed the deputy. "I'll ride along with you."

"No, you won't," said Hatfield. "There's reasons for you stickin' around this part of the country, Cartwright. But let me get on with the rest of it. Montez explained somethin' else, too. It's mighty unusual for anybody to carry deadly poison around with them in packages big enough to cash in four men. But it was natural for Crane to carry sleeping powders. Well, as soon as I saw Montez, I spotted him for a Karankawa.

"The Karanks were the poison people of the Texas Indians — knew how to make and use all kinds of poisons. A Karank can go out on a hillside and get together stuff in no time that'll cash in a roundup. They carry stuff, too. So when Doc figgered the four robbers died of an Indian poison, I naturally thought of Montez, the more so because he recognized me as a man he had seen before there at the ranch house. He might have figured I was a ranger.

"Montez tipped Crane off and he trailed me when I went to the telegraph office. Crane figgered I was gonna horn into his game and went to Holloway. Together, they figgered out that cute little scheme to cash me in there in the saloon."

The lights of Javelina loomed in the distance as the two riders approached the town. They rode slowly, holding their horses to a walk, for Hatfield felt no need for haste now. He was sure that Crane had made his escape, for the time being at least. Still Hatfield had no intention of giving up the chase until the banker was caught.

"Didn't you suspect Angus McPherson at any time?" asked the deputy sheriff.

"Yes," Hatfield replied, "at first because of the shoe marks under the table. They looked like marks made by house slippers. McPherson's cook and wrangler had been gone several days and the floor hadn't been swept. Dust was thick under there, and the prints were plain. But when I got a look at Crane's Congress gaiters, I saw they were shaped and heeled like house slippers, and that helped to tie him up with the business.

"Those sleeve holsters of his interested me right off. I never knew anybody but a professional gambler to carry guns that way. Seemed queer for a respectable banker to do it."

They had swung their horses into the main street of the town and were approaching the Javelina Bank. Cartwright glanced at the building and then uttered a startled exclamation.

"Look!" said the deputy tersely. "There's a light in the window of Crane's private office, and the side door of the bank is open."

"Come on," snapped Hatfield as he reined Goldy and swung out of the saddle. "Let's see what's goin' on in there."

But Wilfred Crane's office was deserted — desk drawers were pulled out, papers scattered about.

"Looks like Crane came back, got what he wanted and flew the coop," said the deputy.

Hatfield went over the office with minute care, and barren results. Crane had covered his tracks well.

"Notion you'll find the bank's affairs sorta stampeded and millin' around; but that's a chore for the county authorities, straightening them out," he told Cartwright.

His gaze swept the office once more as he

stood musing, the concentration furrow deep between his black brows. Suddenly he sniffed sharply and his glance rested on the big pot-bellied stove in the corner. He took a long stride toward it.

"Burning paper," Hatfield muttered as he flung open the door.

The interior of the stove was filled with charred paper. Here and there a last spark winked redly and vanished.

Hatfield stirred the ashes with great caution. A little fluff of feathery particles arose and whisked up the smoke pipe. He peered closer, caught a glimpse of something white. An instant later he was holding an irregular fragment of paper with charred edges.

"A letter," he told Cartwright. "See, there's part of the date mark of the heading. Place it came from is burned away, though. Let's see, now."

Only a single sentence of the missive remained intact, and a few disconnected words.

Yes, could use you and Snoot down here in the Big Bend . . . something big . . . old place . . . Phantoms . . . come . . .

Only a single partly burned capital of the signature remained.

"Looks like an F, or an L, maybe," Cartwright hazarded.

"Doesn't make much difference," Hatfield told him. "Chances are even the full name wouldn't be important."

"Well, it doesn't look to me like much to go on," Cartwright grumbled.

"I've a notion it'll be plenty," Hatfield reassured him. "This is evidently from some jigger Crane was associated with during his gambling days, and this feller has some kettle of stew on the fire and needs Crane's help with the stirring. He's liable to be a big skookum he-wolf in some section. There's a lot of country down in the Big Bend, and it's a salty section, too.

"Lots of places for a stray owlhoot to hole up, but Crane isn't the lone wolf type. He'll land in a town, and towns aren't over plentiful down there. Also, the hangout is somewhere around the Phantom Mountains, the Chisos, as the Mexicans call them. That narrows things down a mite. Yes, I'm pretty certain Crane will head for there, now that he's at loose ends."

The charred paper crumbled to fragments in his fingers. Hatfield threw them back into the stove, dusted off his hands and smiled down at Cartwright.

"Fust off I've got to report back to Cap

McDowell," he said. "There may be some other chore he'll consider more important right now than this one. But sooner or later, I figger ol' Goldy and me will be ambling down into the Big Bend. So if you got any word you'd like to send to *amigo* Crane, we'll try and deliver it."

"I shore wouldn't care to be on the receivin' end of what he'll deliver to Wilfred Crane," Cartwright told himself with emphasis as he watched the tall figure on the golden horse vanish into the distance.

CHAPTER 11
DRUMS OF DEATH

Moonlight like molten silver bathed the Phantom Mountains in ghostly radiance. Crouched with their rugged backs to the ashen band of hurrying water that is the Rio Grande, the mouths of their canyons were as glowering eye sockets under beetling brows. Northward they seemed to stare, those hollow eyes, northward across the desolation of the Big Bend country, northward toward the broad sweep of the Staked Plains.

Grim sentinel of the wastelands, they stood watch on the last frontier, frowning down on the wild range that never had been and never will be disturbed by the plow. Here ranching is supreme. Here, too, roam the deer, the javelin, the panther and the bear. Here grow the greasewood, coarse chino grass, dagger and thorned brush. Here are gloomy caves upon whose walls are painted weird pictures of an age immemorial, whose grim story only the tight-lipped *Indios* of the mountains can decipher.

Here are whispered strange legends. Here live stranger men. Here death walks among the shadows, his bony jaws agape with anticipation. To the east flows the Pecos, "west of which there is no law." To the west is the desert, burning sand and alkali and salt.

In the moonlight the Phantoms crouched and listened — listened to the mutter of drums welling from the depths of a great canyon where white water flowed and black shades clustered. Sinister, ominous were those muttering drums. Over and over they seemed to say:

"We will kill you if we can! We will kill you if we can!"

From the west came a high staccato rattle of question. From the east a deep answering roll. The still air throbbed, the moonlight shimmered, the shadows curdled at the bases of the cliffs. And ever the threatening mutter rose and fell, rose and fell:

"We will kill you if we can! We will kill you if we can!"

To the east of the dark valley where the drums rolled and muttered, a tall man on a great golden horse rode through the moonlight. There were lines of fatigue on Jim

Hatfield's face, for he had followed a long and hard road on the trail of a wanted man. Somewhere in this wild country, the ranger hoped to find Wilfred Crane.

It was a cold trail he was following, Hatfield well knew. Many months had passed since that wild night in the cave near the Guadalupe Mountains, busy months in which things of greater importance than a fugitive killer had occupied Captain Bill McDowell's ace man.

There had been a border war in the making and McDowell could ill afford a troop to cope with the situation at the time. There was just one war going on, however, and Captain Bill decided that one Texas Ranger ought to be enough to handle it — if that ranger was Jim Hatfield.

A bitter feud between rival cattle outfits had required a master hand to smooth out the differences. Two railroads building through the wild lands of Texas got into a row engineered by sinister interests, which for a time threatened to hold up progress. Captain Bill sent the Lone Wolf to "persuade" the interests to desist. Now both railroads were whooping up construction in a spirit of friendly rivalry, which worked to the advantage of Texas and the country as a whole.

All of which had kept the Lone Wolf fairly busy. But he had never forgotten the greedy and conscienceless killer who had tried to add a Texas Ranger to his list of victims. And when opportunity presented, in the line of duty, Hatfield rejoiced that he could again take up his interrupted quest.

Hatfield was tired and the coat of the sorrel was powdered with dust, darkly streaked with dried sweat. But both horse and rider were alert, vigorous, and showed little outward sign of having been on the trail almost continuously for the better part of three days and as many nights.

The moon drifted down the long slant of the western sky, turned from silver to brass, to glowing bronze, to smoldering red-gold. The battlemented crests of the Phantoms were lit with lurid fires and their mighty breasts swathed themselves in robes of royal purple edged with deepest black. Shadowy and unreal appeared those somber mountains, shouldering against the sky, pushing back the stars and yawning a grim grave mouth to receive the dying moon.

Small wonder that the followers of Cabeza de Vaca, in the days when Spain was mighty and Texas a land of mystery and the unknown, stared askance at the grim crags and pinnacles that loomed ominously before their startled eyes and muttered between bearded lips:

"Chisos!" Phantoms, unreal.

Still Jim Hatfield rode westward, following a trail that swung dizzily between two eternities, plotting his course by the great wheeling map of the sky. Suddenly he raised his head, listening.

Goldy heard it, too, that eerie whispering which drifted from out of the black dark; he pricked nervous ears.

"Drums!" muttered Hatfield. "Again! Long way off, but no mistaking them. Talking drums!"

Intently he listened, while the horse's irons rang loudly on the stony soil, the wind soughed mournfully through the pass and the stars turned from gold to silver and from great glowing sparks to gleaming pinpoints of light.

"But *that* isn't drums!" Hatfield abruptly exclaimed.

One slim hand dropped instinctively to a black gun butt. His lithe figure straightened from its careless lounge, grew tense, alert. The lean hawk face tightened to immobility until it seemed hewn from dark granite. The long green eyes narrowed the merest trifle.

Louder grew the swiftly approaching sound, a rhythmic clicking that swelled to a low thunder. The Lone Wolf knew it to be the beat of flying hoofs on the hard trail. There was a frantic note in the sound, as if the racing horse were fleeing from some pursuing terror. Sheer panic, and retching fatigue, emphasized in the sudden stumbling falter of the drumming irons, and the instantly increased tempo of the beat.

"If something isn't herding that jigger along, my name isn't Jim Hatfield," the ranger muttered. "Goldy, let's you and me sorta sidle over and hug the cliff wall till he shows up. It's an almighty long drop to the ground from the lip of this sky-climbing trail."

The golden horse snorted agreement and as Hatfield reined him, he snugged against the cliff, ears pricked, nostrils flaring slightly, great brown eyes staring expectantly toward the bulge in the cliff a score of yards ahead, around which the trail swung loosely, dipping slightly toward the rock wall, its far edge ragged and crumbling.

"If he doesn't slow up, he'll go over the edge shore as shootin'," Hatfield muttered. "Gosh all hemlock! Listen to him come!"

With the abruptness of a bursting shell, things happened. There was a crash of hoofs, a scraping and a screeching as the worn steel of the shoes slipped on the stone, a popping of saddle leather and a jangle of threshing stirrups. Grotesque, distorted in the moonlight, looming gigantic, a great black horse burst around the bulge.

Hatfield had a fantastic glimpse of rolling eyes, flaring red nostrils and foam-flecked, tossing mane.

Too late the maddened animal realized his danger. He tried to swerve, leaning far inward, his straining muscles leaping out in ropes beneath his glossy hide. But his irons slipped on the stone, his feet shot from under him. He gave one horrible wailing scream and plunged over the crumbling lip of the trail. Down toward the reaching fangs of stone nigh a thousand feet below.

The crash of his falling body came back to the listener on the trail as the tiniest of sounds.

Jim Hatfield raised a bronzed hand and wiped his suddenly moist brow. The golden horse exhaled his breath in a quivering snort. Then he whinnied plaintively, with ears erect and quivering.

"Yeah, he's gone, feller," Hatfield muttered. "Nothin' left of him but busted bones and sausage meat after that drop. Now what in blazes is this all about? Let's you and me go and see."

He urged the golden horse around the

bulge and rode swiftly up the winding track, searching the trail ahead with eyes that missed no detail. That there was danger somewhere ahead, or at the best, grim tragedy, Jim Hatfield knew, for although the fleeing horse had worn both bridle and saddle, he had carried no rider on his back.

The trail swerved abruptly, narrowed, edged around a cliff that seemed bent on shouldering it off into space. It straightened and the moonlight slanted misty beams across its surface. They fell on a huddled something a few score feet ahead.

"It's him!" Hatfield exclaimed. "Hold it, hoss! He must be —"

Crash!

From the huddled form gushed a lance of orange flame. Goldy shied as the bullet screeched past scant inches from his black ear.

In a bewildering ripple of movement, Hatfield was out of the saddle and crouched in the deeper shadow of the cliff, both long guns out and jutting forward. But he held his fire, gambling on the injured man's inability to line a sight.

"Hold it, feller, I'm not on the prod against you!" Hatfield called, and instantly shifted his position.

Only a gurgling moan and a horrible

unintelligible gabble of sound replied. The figure on the trail writhed, stiffened, relaxed, and was strangely still.

Ranger Jim Hatfield had before now seen men lie thus starkly still. Face bleak in the moonlight, he stood up and holstered his guns. Without hesitation or hurry he strode forward and knelt beside the motionless form. He had judged correctly that motionless silence. The man was dead.

Hatfield peered closer into the distorted face. The man's mouth was gaping open and from it still welled a sluggish flow of blood. Hatfield stared, and started back with an exclamation. The mouth was a gruesome empty cavity, blood-smeared, horrible. *The dead man's tongue had been torn from his jaws!*

A swift examination showed the immediate cause of the man's death. He had been shot through the body, high up over the heart. Only a drop or two of blood had welled from the small blue hole in his left breast.

"Internal bleeding," Hatfield deduced. "And he shore couldn't have come far. It doesn't seem he coulda rode at all, the shape he was in. He's been sliced to bits with small knives, I'd say. Yaqui knives, from the looks of the cuts. But I never heard tell of Yaquis yanking a man's tongue out. They allus make it a point to keep him so he can yell and cry. Nice section I'm heading into!"

Hatfield stood up, peering, listening. There was no movement on the moonlit trail ahead, and he could see for nearly half a mile. Nor was there any sound.

Then suddenly there *was* sound — an eerie muttering. A rasping whisper which swelled to a staccato rattle as the wind soughed down the pass. It seemed to the listener that in the quick beat of the "talking drums" there was a note of fiendish satisfaction and triumph. With a final deep roll the sound ceased, and only the lonely murmur of the wind threaded the dark blanket of the silence.

CHAPTER 12
THE DEVIL'S CORRAL

Sprawled in the lap of the Phantoms, not far from the awful gorge which bounds the Big Bend country, the cow and mining town of Coma greeted the sun with a bleary face. The slopes above the gaunt mine buildings were thickly grown with the thorny evergreen trees from which the town derived its name.

The *Escondida* Mine dominated the town. As its name denoted, this old Spanish gold mine had lain "hidden" in the brush for centuries, its dark mouth finally stumbled upon by a wandering prospector. The Escondida developed a crumbly gravel which released gold in paying quantities. Thereupon old Mike Shaw, the prospector, prospered, and so did Coma.

Coma hadn't been doing bad as it was. Much of the Big Bend country is bitter desert and wasteland, but not all. There are stretches of fine grazing land, well wooded, abundantly watered.

Here, as on the rolling plains farther east, grow needle and wheat grasses, and the curly mesquite rich in the distilled spirit of the blazing Texas sun and the sweet rains of the dry country, which plumps out the ribs of truculent steers and turns staid old horses into frisking hellions.

On either side of where Coma huddles in the shadow of the towering slopes, the Phantoms send out long granite claws — claws that are like to the outstretched paws of a crouching lion. And, a sleeping lamb curled within the menacing paws of the lion, a great valley curves west and northwest.

So wide is the valley that from its center, where brawls a turbulent stream, the cliffs on either hand, tall and mighty though they are, grow misty with distance. On cloudy days they veil themselves in swirling mists and vanish altogether, to burst suddenly through the sunwash like very Phantoms, their name.

On and on, mile upon misty mile, stretches Mescalero Valley, until the grim crags of the Cienagos spire into the western sky at no great distance and the desert halts the fertile country with a bleached and bony hand.

There are ranches in Mescalero Valley, big

ranches, and a few little ones. The XT, the C Bar O, the Bowtie, and the Arrow, among others.

Most of them date back to the days before Mexican independence, and some are still owned by proud descendants of the old Dons who came from Spain to seek fortune and adventure in this far-flung domain of the Spanish king.

The drives to the east and north have always passed through Coma to reach the markets beyond the Texas border, and later the shipping pens of the railroad. Because of these drives, Coma first came into being, and because of them Coma became a hell town of the border.

The Chisos Trail from Mexico also loops past Coma in its shifty crawl to the north and the Chisos did its bit to enliven Coma and make of it a place avoided by the peace-loving and the timid.

Old Mike Shaw and his gold mine merely stepped up the tempo a bit and provided a new flow of hard money. Other gold deposits tapped farther back in the hills also did their part, until Coma, which had formerly growled the note of a truculent bobcat, developed the full-throated roar of a mountain lion on the prod.

The trail — a fork of the Chisos — to the

railroad town, beyond the Phantoms and forty miles to the northeast, clings to the side of the swelling slope in whose shadow Coma lies, climbs sharply enough to make a herd pant and bawl, and dips over the lofty crest. It curves close to the "diggin's" of the Escondida Mine and tumbles down into the town with a dusty sigh of relief.

With the morning sun burning brightly at his back and still making a hard climb of it up the steep slant of the eastern sky, Ranger Jim Hatfield rode down the curving trail. Far below he could see the huddle and sprawl of Coma, with the gaunt mine buildings still washed in the retreating shadow. As he drew near, he could hear sounds of activity along the slope lying ahead.

"Looks like they're opening a new mine tunnel there," he mused, "and having to do a heap of shoring up. Must be pretty crumbly soil there, shattered rock and such stuff."

As he approached still closer to the scene of activity, his dark brows drew together slightly and he shook his black head.

"Those supporting beams are set at too wide an angle," he muttered. "That's gambling on trouble, pertickler if a hard and sudden rain happens to come on."

He eyed the proceedings with the eye of an engineer, rather than of the cowhand his dress proclaimed. For Jim Hatfield, before the tragic death of his father due to business reversals which had resulted in the loss of the elder Hatfield's prosperous ranch, had had better than two years in engineering college. And would doubtless have gone on and completed his course had not the murder of his father by wideloopers sent him on the vengeance trail, and thence into the Texas Rangers.

As it happened, Hatfield's predicted "trouble" didn't wait on the rain. Above where the shoring for the new tunnel was taking form, men were busy clearing away the growth and removing boulders, of which there were plenty. The removal of one of the big chunks of rock suddenly started a shifting and sliding of a number of its fellows.

Before Goldy had time to snort his alarm at the abrupt racket, a respectable slide was roaring down the slope. It hit the shoring with a crash and instantly there was a wild pandemonium of splintering timbers, thudding rock falls, yells of terror and howls of pain.

A huge mushroom of dust billowed up and covered the whole scene of destruction. Before it had settled enough for Hatfield to see what all had happened, there arose from its midst a volley of piercing screams which swiftly died to gabbling moans and gasping whimpers.

"On, Goldy!" Hatfield shouted.

The big sorrel stretched his long neck and fairly raced down the trail. His rider left the saddle while he was in full stride and the golden horse skittered to a snorting halt. Hatfield ran swiftly to the scene of the accident, forcing his way through a straggle of brush.

The dust was lifting, and the workmen who had fled the avalanche of earth and rock were scrambling back up the slope, shouting excitedly.

There was good cause for excitement. The inadequate shoring had failed to withstand the blow from above. The too widely angled supporting beams had skidded and crumpled and the whole mass had crashed down upon the workmen beneath.

A single glance told Hatfield that the unfortunates who had borne the full brunt of the fall were beyond help, crushed and mangled under tons of stone. But in the fringe of the rubble, pinned by a heavy beam across their chests, were two men whose agonized writhing and gasping moans told they were still alive.

"But they won't be for long," Hatfield

muttered. "The rock on top of that beam is sinking it deeper and deeper into the earth and increasing the pressure on them."

Their fellow workmen also realized the danger. They swarmed over the huge mound, tearing at the rock and earth with ineffectual hands and equally ineffectual picks and bars. Others tried desperately to lift the beam from the two victims. But the manner in which the timber was jammed against the splintered shoring prevented more than one pair of hands at a time from getting a purchase on the free end. And the weight was far beyond the strength of a single man to lift.

All this Hatfield realized in one swift glance. He whistled shrilly, a piercing urgent note. Instantly there was a crashing in the growth and a moment later the great sorrel horse slid to a halt beside his master.

Hatfield's lariat was looped over the saddle horn. He grasped it, slipped the noosed end over the end of the beam and glanced about. A little distance down the slope and slightly to one side was a stout tree. One thick branch protruded parallel to the end of the beam. With a jerk of his wrist, Hatfield sent the free end of the rope spinning over the limb to dangle loosely on the far side. He swung into the saddle.

"All right, you fellows, stand in the clear!" Hatfield shouted to the workmen, and sent Goldy down the slope. He caught the dangling end of the rope as he passed beneath it and took a couple of dallies about the saddle horn. He steadied the golden horse, checked his stride.

"Take it easy, feller," he cautioned. "Don't snap the twine."

Goldy, who knew perfectly the art of checking a fleeing steer, and turning him a flip-flop if necessary, tightened the rope with just the proper amount of force. The taut line hummed like a harp string. Goldy bunched his feet, resisted with all his mighty strength, and snorted angrily as he was hurled back. He took a little slack, swelled his great chest and lunged.

There was a rattling crash, the thud of falling rock and earth. Goldy floundered forward a couple of steps. Hatfield instantly checked him and he stood straining against the humming rope.

A chorus of triumphant shouts told Hatfield that the victims were hauled free. He eased the sorrel back and loosened his dallies. Then he swung to the ground and walked back, expertly coiling his rope and flipping the noose free from the beam end. He knelt by the side of the injured men, who lay moaning.

"Some busted ribs but no lung punctures, so far as I can make out," was his verdict after a swift examination. "Make stretchers outa poles thrust through coat sleeves and carry 'em down to a doctor," he ordered the workmen. "Pronto, now — they need attention. And the rest of your fellers had better start getting those bodies from under that mess."

The workers hurried to obey. "You sure come along in the nick of time, cowboy," said a brawny individual, wiping sweat from his face. "And that was sure fast thinkin' on your part," he added admiringly. "If it hadn't been for you, we'd never have got poor Pete and Alex out in time."

Hatfield nodded, and was about to reply, when a rousing commotion on the far side of the mound of rubble denoted another act in the drama. A high, tremulous, but singularly fierce and compelling voice was heard shouting.

"Git out! Git out! You're fired, I tell you! Git out! When I put a man to bossin' a job, I want him to be able to boss it, not make a hash of it. You're one fool mine foreman, you are! Look what you've went and done! Git out!"

Hatfield strode around the splintered

shoring and beheld a little old man with flaring whiskers, who could not weigh over a hundred pounds soaking wet. A wizened figure of wrath, he faced a big-shouldered man with a sullen, mutinous face who glared angrily down at him.

As Hatfield approached, he took a menacing stride toward the little man, but the oldster sturdily held his place.

"Git out!" he repeated.

"I weren't to blame," rumbled the big man. "Them fellers up above loosened that stuff and sent it down on top of us."

"And the way you built that shorin', a coupla rocks squashed it flat!" raged the other. "You went and murdered three good men, mebbe five!"

At this indictment, the big man gave a bellow of anger. He swung at the oldster with a fist like a sunburned ham. The blow, had it landed, might well have broken the other's neck.

But it didn't land. Fingers like slim rods of nickel steel, clamped on the hairy wrist, deflected the blow and swung the big man halfway around to face Jim Hatfield.

"He isn't half yore size," the Texas Ranger protested mildly, "and he's nigh onto forty years older."

The big man roared again. "You blankety-blank!" he howled.

He lunged fiercely at Hatfield. The blow was blocked before it had traveled six inches and as Hatfield let go the other's wrist, he did so with a wrench that sent the big man reeling back.

"Take it easy," Hatfield cautioned in the same deceptively mild drawl. "Take it easy, feller, I'm not on the prod against you."

But the big man was beside himself. Bellowing curses, he rushed, both thick arms flailing. Hatfield sighed resignedly, weaved aside and hit him with a fist that was like to the slim, steely face of a sledgehammer.

The big man sailed through the air as if he had taken unto himself wings, hit the ground with a thud, and stayed there. Hatfield turned his glance on the little man with the whiskers.

"Good work, son," the oldster applauded, "thank-e! But I'da handled him," he added truculently, glaring at the fallen man, who was groaning with returning consciousness. "The blankety-blank! Will you look at the mess he made of that job! What do you think of that?"

Hatfield ran his eyes up the scarred slope.

"I think," he said quietly, "that you had better give him his job back when he comes to."

"What's that?" bawled the old-timer. "What's that? Why —"

"You handed an engineer's chore to a drift boss, the way I see it," Hatfield interrupted the tirade. "Did *you* figger the way that slope would act when you started work on it?"

"Nope, I didn't," the other admitted.

"The angle of his support beams was too wide," Hatfield explained. "They were just about right for ordinary conditions, but conditions here aren't ordinary. Nope, I wouldn't blame that jigger too much, if I was you."

The oldster glared at the big man, who was sitting up, rubbing his swollen jaw.

"Do you hear that, Harper?" he barked. "This overlong hellion says I didn't have no business firin' you for a mistake I made myself!"

The big man scowled from one to the other and seemed about to make an angry reply. But before he could speak, Jim Hatfield smiled down at him from his great height, his teeth flashing white and even in his bronzed face and his green eyes sunny as summer seas. That smile abruptly transformed his stern face into something wonderfully pleasant.

In spite of himself, the big man grinned

reply. He leaped lightly to his feet and somewhat sheepishly held out his hand.

"Reckon I went off sorta half-cocked," he admitted. "Glad you kept me from doin' somethin' I'd been plumb 'shamed of afterward." He felt of his jaw and his grin widened. "Feller, you're good," he said admiringly. "I ain't been hit so hard since my mother-in-law left me to run off with a sheepherder!"

Hatfield took the proffered hand in a firm grip.

"All right! All right!" barked the irascible oldster. "Stop foolin' around and git on the job, Harper. Git them bodies out."

"Okay, Uncle Mike," rumbled the other as he turned to the mass of debris.

The old man was regarding Hatfield with a truculent eye.

"Jest how would *you* go about drivin' that tunnel?" he demanded.

Hatfield eyed the gravelly slope for a moment.

"I wouldn't," he replied briefly.

The old man seemed on the verge of another explosion, but restrained himself with evident effort.

"Then how in the blankety-blank would you git the gravel out?" he demanded. "It's

121

down deep that there's gold in payin' quantities."

Hatfield turned and thoughtfully gazed across the slope to where, less than a quarter of a mile distant, the feathery plume of a high waterfall showed white against the dark mouth of a canyon.

"I'd use that water over there to get the gravel out," he said.

At this remark, the intermittent geyser of Uncle Mike's wrath spouted up again with scalding steam, brimstone and blue flame. Hatfield waited patiently for the exhibition to cease, which it finally did when Uncle Mike ran out of breath. Then he proceeded to elucidate:

"The floor of that canyon is considerably higher than most of this gravel slope, and that stream runs mighty swift. Because of that you could get a good pressure over here without having to resort to compressors or pumps. Didn't you ever hear or read of hydraulic mining?"

Uncle Mike profanely admitted he had "heerd somethin' about some newfangled contraption," but opined he "didn't believe that the blankety-blank gimmick would work."

"It's not pertickler new, and it works," Hatfield told him. "A gravel drift like this is made to order for hydraulics. It's a sight cheaper method than tunneling and shoring. Yes, I know the old Spaniards tunneled and shored through gravel drifts, but they didn't have any choice. They didn't know anything about hydraulic mining — hadn't been invented in their day.

"Here you could set up 'giants' with nozzles that give you an eight-inch stream of water and knock that gravel down easy. The cost would be nothing compared to what tunneling and shoring would be."

"Shoring is danged expensive," Uncle Mike admitted. "That's one of the reasons I'm givin' over my ol' Escondida Mine 'crost there to the south for these new diggin's, oncet I get 'em operatin'. Plenty of good dirt in the lower Escondida levels, but it's costin' too danged much to git it out.

"I was lucky to file over here too when I hit on that ol' lost mine. It's the same gravel belt, but there ain't no surface indications of gold and nobody ever figgered it was wuth a hoot."

He pondered for a moment, then suddenly fixed Hatfield with his shrewd old eyes.

"S'posin' I decide to put in them contraptions, will you take hold and git 'em set up and starting operatin'?" he demanded. "You 'pear to know what you're gabbin' about."

Hatfield did not reply at once. The concentration furrow between his black brows deepened, a sure sign that the man a stern old Lieutenant of Rangers named the Lone Wolf was doing some hard thinking.

"I was sorta figgering on trying to drop my twine on a job of ridin' somewhere up the valley," he remarked at length.

"I'll pay you a sight more'n them cattle fellers'll pay you to chase bulls," Uncle Mike shot at him. "Want to talk it over?"

"Tell you what," Hatfield replied, "I got a little chore down to the sheriff's office. Coma is the county seat, isn't it? And after that I'll think the thing over and give you an answer after I tie onto a little shut-eye. I'm so sleepy right now I can't think straight. And my belly's cravin' feed."

"Okay," grunted Uncle Mike. "Shaw's my name. Mike Shaw. Drop into the office down to the Escondida buildin' down in town when you're a mind to talk business. By the way, there's a good sleepin' place right across the street from the mine buildin'. Tell 'em I sent you. Ted Harper, the feller you gave the lickin' to, and some of the boys sleep there. Stalls right across the street for yore hoss."

CHAPTER 13
DEATH STRIKES AGAIN

Hatfield rode the two miles to town and found the sheriff's office without difficulty. The sheriff was in, seated at a table, glowering at some papers. He was long and lanky, grizzled and mustached, and had a cantankerous look about him. A big nickel shield was pinned to his sagging vest; a heavy gun hung at one scrawny hip. He regarded Hatfield with a cold blue eye.

"Well, what do *you* want?" he demanded, with a profane designation as to the region.

"Just dropped in to make a report," Hatfield replied. "There's a dead man in the trail about seventeen miles east of here."

The sheriff's chair jerked back with creaking legs.

"What's that?" he demanded.

Hatfield repeated his message, and added details. The sheriff swore until he was out of breath.

"Injuns again!" he bellowed. "Them

125

blankety-blank-blanks! They're gettin' wuss and wuss. We're in for a plumb uprisin' here."

"Funny," commented Hatfield, "I thought all the hostiles were cleared outa this district fifteen, twenty years back."

"That's what everybody claims to think!" fumed the sheriff. "That's what Bill Mc-Dowell said when I writ him askin' for a company of Texas Rangers to come over here and scatter the ornery hellions. Said local authority oughta be able to handle the few Injuns what were left here. Opined it warn't nothin' but a coupla bucks with a snootful of red-eye actin' up!"

"Coupla bucks, hell! As many as fifty of the black-faced sidewinders has been seen ridin' together, and all packin' good guns, too. And most any night you hear the war drums beat back in the hills."

"Black-faced?" Hatfield mused. "That must mean Apaches or Yaquis. You shore about this, Sheriff?"

"Am I shore!" bellowed the old officer. "Say, who the blankety-blank are you to come here askin' me if I'm shore about somethin'!"

He glared up at the Lone Wolf, but something in the steady gaze of the long green eyes that met his so unwaveringly caused

126

him to shift his own glance, fumble with his hands and mutter under his mustache.

"I'm sorta put out, feller," he said apologetically at length. "Things has been happenin' too fast hereabouts of late, and this news you brung in don't help me to feel any better."

He stood up, hitching his gun belt higher about his lean waist.

"I'll get me a buckboard and a coupla deputies and ride out there," he announced. "You drop into the office late this evening' to identify the corpse as the one you saw, and then we'll have another talk. You figger on hanging' around in this district?"

"Mebbe," Hatfield replied bitterly. "I'll be here when you get back, anyhow."

He did not mention to Sheriff Dobson that he had read the letter the latter wrote to McDowell, and listened to the grim old Ranger captain's comments.

"There's somethin' off-color over there," Captain Bill rumbled. "Clate Dobson ain't the sort to bawl-beller jest to let off wind. Clate ain't over heft on brains, but he's a good man and honest. Jim, I figger they don't nobody much know you down in that section, so you jest sashay down and look things over. If it's jest a coupla dozen bucks fired up with rattlesnake juice, comb their wool down for them and hustle back. If it's somethin' really serious, hang on till it's cleaned up."

"Fine," Hatfield had replied. "Been hoping for a chance to get down into that section. You'll rec'lect, suh, that's where that hellion Wilfred Crane is supposed to have trailed his rope to. Or at least I figgered as much when I found that scrap of a letter written by somebody, in which was discussed the Big Bend country as if he knew it well and had friends there. Fact is, I plumb got a hunch I'll find him there."

"Yore hunches have a habit of workin'," McDowell admitted. He stared curiously at the stern hawk face of the Lone Wolf. The green eyes were cold, somber, the rather wide mouth hard set.

"You don't never forget, do you?" he remarked. "Been quite a spell since Crane give you the slip and there's been a hefty herd of mighty interestin' cattle slid through the chute in the meanwhile, but you still kept that banker-gambler hellion in mind, eh? Well, hope you have luck with him; got a notion you will."

With which Captain Bill dismissed the matter along with his troop lieutenant and ace man, confident that no matter what might develop in that land of blood and desolation, the Big Bend, the Lone Wolf would prove competent to cope with the situation.

Hatfield found a comfortable stall and a nosebag for Goldy. When the sorrel had been properly cared for, he repaired to a small eating house nearby and stowed away a few helpings of grub. The bunkhouse old Mike Shaw recommended proved satisfactory and Hatfield went to bed. When he awoke some time after dark, he had decided to accept old Mike Shaw's offer.

"Will give me an excuse for hangin' around here," he mused, "and more chance to wander about on my own than a job of ridin' would."

Hatfield ate his breakfast and went to the sheriff's office. He found great excitement prevailing there. A number of big-boned cattlemen were present, grouped around the body the sheriff had brought in several hours earlier.

They eyed Hatfield coldly and he sensed more than a trace of suspicion in their glances as Dobson performed a rapid-fire of introduction. The sheriff's next words enlightened him as to their attitude.

"This feller you found," said Dobson, "was Bruce Ralston, one of the biggest spread owners in Mescalero Valley. He'd been missin' several days, but folks figgered he was stayin' over in Welch, the railroad town over east. How come him to be out there on the Coma Trail, and ridin' east, is beyond me. You shore he was ridin' east, Hatfield?"

The Texas Ranger nodded. "I tried to figger where he mighta come from," he added, "but it was night time and the moon was pretty high down, and there's any number of canyons and arroyos opening onto the trail 'tween here and where I found him. I figgered he come outa one of those canyons, but there was no way of telling which one."

"And you say you run onto him jest t'other side Talkin' Water Canyon?" asked Joe Hayes, a hard-faced young man with broad shoulders and abnormally long arms.

"Didn't say," Hatfield replied. "I don't know one canyon from another in this district. I'm a stranger here."

Hayes grunted something under his breath. "Too damn many strangers in this district of late," he remarked with meaning.

"Uh-huh, hard to keep an eye on 'em," Hatfield agreed mildly, "or to be shore who *they're* keeping an eye on."

Joe Hayes stared uncertainly, mouthed something unintelligible and appeared at a loss just how to answer the apparently innocent remark. Before he could make up his mind, Henry Lyons, a swarthily handsome man with somber dark eyes, voiced a protest.

"You're talking out of turn, Hayes," he remarked, a trifle contemptuously. "This kind of gabble doesn't get us anywhere."

Hayes grumbled under his breath, but subsided. A tall old fellow, Train Beverly, owner of the big XT, took up the conversation.

"This jest about tetches the limit," he said. "I'm in favor of organizin' a vigilante committee and cleanin' them hellions out proper."

"Clean out who proper?" barked the sheriff.

"The Injuns," Beverly replied vaguely.

The sheriff snorted his disgust. "You gotta ketch Injuns, or anybody else, 'fore you clean 'em out," he declared. "Ain't nobody hit onto any Injun settlement hereabouts. Yeah, I know, reports has come in of bands ridin', but can any of you hostile gents tell me where to tie onto one of them bands?

"And so far as that goes, they don't nobody know for shore that Injuns is 'sponsible for the trouble hereabouts. Some of the things what have happened 'pear to me to be a mite out of the ordinary in the Injun line of work."

The hard-faced Hayes suddenly turned to Hatfield. "Stranger," he growled, "you ain't said so, but I'm willing to bet you heard drums in the hills last night!"

Hatfield nodded slowly. "I did," he admitted, "talking drums, if I'm not mistaken."

"See!" Hayes exclaimed triumphantly. "Every time some hell breaks loose, the damn drums talk. It happened when Warner was killed. They talked when those two XT hands were found pegged out on ant hills, and when the 8 Bar W ranch house was burned. Drums every damn time! Talkin' drums!"

There was a general nodding of heads. Hatfield's black brows drew together slightly, but he made no comment. A little while later the meeting broke up, the cattlemen going their various ways.

Hatfield was left alone with the sheriff. The old officer regarded him with a peculiar expression on his leathery face.

"Feller," he said, "I didn't bring it up 'fore now, 'cause them fellers were in too much of a wranglin' mood to need anythin' else to argufy over, but there's somethin' I want to speak to you about. As I rec'lect, you said Ralston took a shot at you 'fore he cashed in, right? Well, when we found his body, he warn't wearin' no belts, and there warn't a sign of a gun nowhere around."

Hatfield countered with a question: "What kinda guns did he generally pack?"

The sheriff's grizzled brows drew together. "Don't see what difference that makes," he growled, "but Bruce allus leathered a old Smith & Wesson Russian model, a forty-four. But I tell you there warn't no gun on him," he added.

"Nope, I reckon not," Hatfield agreed, " 'cause" — he reached inside his shirt — "here it is."

With that he laid a short-barreled six on the table.

The sheriff snatched it up, glared at it. "This ain't no Smith forty-four, this ain't Ralston's gun!" he declared accusingly.

Hatfield nodded agreement. "I figgered as much from the looks of him," he replied. "I thought it a mite strange for an old-timer like Ralston showed plain he was, to be packing a new model thirty-two-twenty with a short barrel. That's a shoulder-holster gun, and belt marks showed plain on Ralston's shirt. That's why I brought it along — figgered such an uncommon calibre and model was wuth hangin' onto under the circumstances."

"That's right," agreed the sheriff, "but

why didn't you hand it to me this morning?"

"Wanted to see if there would be any remark about that feller not packing any gun when you found him. You see, I figger Ralston took this gun offa one of the hellions what did him in, when he broke away from them, like he musta done. Do you know anybody in this section who packs a gun of this calibre? They're mighty uncommon west of the Pecos."

The sheriff shook his head. "But I'll shore try and find out," he declared. "You thunk up something' there, feller. You got the makin's of a good peace officer or I'm a heap mistook."

"You didn't go down into the canyon and look at Ralston's horse, did you?" Hatfield asked. "I was wondering if there is a way into that canyon."

"We didn't go down," Sheriff Dobson admitted. "Was gettin' late and it's a big chore, hafta make a five-mile ride back east to begin with, and then another five miles or so up the canyon. Rough goin'. Why?"

"The horse might be wearing a brand," Hatfield replied. "Not that it would necessarily mean much," he added. "Branded horses are widelooped same as unbranded ones. But then again it might."

134

"I'll make that trip come tomorrer," said the sheriff. "Now about this gun —"

"Put it in yore safe," Hatfield advised. "I see you got a strong looking one on t'other side the room under the window. I'll drop in again tomorrow evening in case you wanta talk to me again. Right now I gotta little chore to do."

The sheriff nodded and Hatfield left him seated before the table, staring at the odd-calibred gun.

The Texas Ranger walked leisurely along the dimly lighted street, pausing at the corner to roll a cigarette with the slim fingers of his left hand. He had just lighted the brain tablet when he heard, back the way he had come, the sound of a shot, muffled as if the gun had been fired inside a room. He hesitated a moment, and as he did so, there came to his ears a patter of swift feet dying quickly into the distance.

"Sounded like it was back by the sheriff's office," he muttered. "Mebbe I'd better slide back and take a look-see."

He retraced his steps, paused before the sheriff's office and glanced through the door, which stood slightly ajar. Sheriff Dobson still sat at the table, facing the open window on the far side of the room, apparently deep in thought.

Hatfield half turned away, when something unnatural about the way the sheriff's head lolled to one side gave him pause. He shoved open the door and stepped into the room. A single glance at close range was enough.

The old peace officer was dead, shot through the heart!

CHAPTER 14
"WITH THE
SUBSTANCE OF MY SOUL"

Hatfield's gaze flickered across the room.

"Stuck the gun through the window and let him have it," he muttered.

He swept the room with an all-embracing glance. Everything appeared the same as when he had left it but a few minutes before. No! not everything! The odd-calibred gun was no longer lying on the table.

It was nowhere in sight. Hatfield peered under the table, behind the sheriff's chair. The safe was shut and locked and he felt certain that the sheriff had not had time to open it and place the gun inside.

"Nope, it's gone," he concluded. "I've a big hunch that's what the hellion killed Dobson for. He wanted that gun — wanted it mighty bad. Must have been hanging around outside that window and listenin' to us talk. Didn't want that gun to stay here, and didn't want Dobson goin' around making inquiries about it."

Hatfield turned at a sudden sound outside. Feet pounded on the porch. Young Joe Hayes and Walt Wagner, the fat deputy, stepped through the door. They took in the situation at a glance.

Hayes' hand flickered toward his gun. It froze on the butt, the muscles of his arm bulging with strain, his face darkening with anger.

But he had sense enough to respect the twin black muzzles glowering at him. Jim Hatfield's double draw had been as the flicker of a rattler's fangs in the death stroke. His green eyes, cold as a frozen wave, regarded the pair.

Wagner slowly raised his hands, shoulder high. Hayes, with the greatest care, let go his gun and followed suit.

"You can't get away with it, feller. We'll ketch you 'fore you make the border," Wagner quavered.

" 'Less he aims to do us in too, 'fore he starts," Hayes said in a voice that denoted he believed that only too probable. His black glare met Hatfield's gaze unflinchingly, however.

Wagner's face whitened and he moistened his lips with a nervous tongue.

"I don't aim to do anybody in, and I'm

not going anywhere," Hatfield quietly reassured them. "I'm just aiming to keep you
from doing something you'd be sorry about
afterwards. Did you hear the shot that
cashed in the sheriff?"

"I heered it," Wagner admitted. "I was jest
roundin' the corner below here."

"Me, too," was Hayes' grudging reply. "I
was comin' outa the Swallerfork saloon
'crost the way. What difference does that
make?"

"Only this," Hatfield replied. "I'd hardly
have had time to clean my guns, would I?
Here."

He flipped the big Colts in his hands and
held them out, butts first.

"Look 'em over," he invited.

Lowering his hands, Wagner did so. Hayes
leaned over his shoulder and watched.

"Reckon that clears you, feller," Wagner
admitted, returning the guns. "They shore
ain't been shot off recent."

" 'Less he used another gun!" Hayes
growled suspiciously.

"And swallered it after I used it!" Hatfield
interjected, a note of exasperation in his
voice. "S'pose you look around the office
and outside the door and window." He holstered his guns and raised his hands above
his head. "And look me over, too," he added.

Hayes bent a long stare upon him and shook his head, still grudgingly.

"Reckon you didn't have anything to do with it," he grunted, "but, feller, you shore got a plumb gift for showin' up where bodies happen to be!"

"Speakin' of bodies," put in Wagner, "let's lay pore ol' Clate on the bunk over there. It gives me the creeps lookin' at him settin' in his chair with his haid hangin' sideways."

The others offered no objection and Hayes and Hatfield assisted the deputy in transferring the body to the couch. They straightened the limbs decently, folded the gnarled hands and stepped back.

Hatfield suddenly pointed to the sheriff's chair. "There's the bullet that did for him!" he exclaimed. "Passed right through his body and brought up in the chair back."

"Well, I'll be damned!" muttered Wagner.

The deputy strode to the chair and tried to loosen the battered bit of lead, without success. Then Hayes tried and likewise failed.

"Hafta get a chisel and pry it loose, I reckon," Hayes growled. "Mebbe I can get it out with my knife."

"Let me have a try," said Hatfield.

He gripped the protruding base of the slug between his thumb and forefinger. The two

140

watchers saw great muscles leap out along his arm like taut ropes. The sleeve of his shirt suddenly split from wrist to elbow and the bullet came out of the wood!

"Good gosh!" breathed Wagner. "Feller, I'd shore hate to have yore fingers round my windpipe!" He peered at the battered bullet that Hatfield laid upon the table. "What a mite of a slug!" he wondered. "Why, it ain't no bigger around than a buckshot!"

"Easy to see it didn't come outa one of my forty-fives," Hatfield remarked grimly.

"Nor outa any hawglaig I ever seed round these diggin's," Wagner declared with conviction. "What calibre is that, anyway?"

Hayes examined the bullet. " 'Bout a thirty-two, I'd say," he offered.

"Yes," Hatfield agreed softly, "or a thirty-two-twenty."

Hayes shot him a quick glance, but made no comment.

"I'll go tell the coroner," Wagner said. "Doc McChesney is shore gettin' plenty business of late. Gents, there's gonna be hell over this. Ol' Clate was mighty well liked in this district. Hatfield, we'll want you at the inquest tomorrow. Will be a double inquest, I reckon, and you're sorta star witness to both."

141

Wagner hesitated a moment, glanced thoughtfully toward the jail cells behind the office, rubbed his chin. Whatever was in his mind, he evidently decided to refrain from putting it into action.

Hatfield's lips quirked slightly at the corners as he rightly interpreted Wagner's glance.

"Okay, I'll be there," Hatfield said. "Now I got a little chore to 'tend to, if you're all through with me."

Hatfield had no trouble locating the Escondida building and the office.

"Well, you took yore time gittin' here!" old Mike greeted him cantankerously.

In a few words Hatfield acquainted him with the death of the sheriff. He expected the news to elicit another explosion, but instead Shaw sat strangely quiet, staring straight ahead of him.

"Pore ol' Clate," he said at length, "pore ol' Clate." He turned suddenly to face the Texas Ranger.

"Hatfield," he said, "that's yore name, ain't it — I got a notion I'm to blame for all this."

Hatfield glanced at him in surprise. "How you figger that?" he asked curiously.

Uncle Mike did not reply at once, and

when he did, it was in the form of a question.

"Hatfield," he said slowly, "do you believe in cusses?"

The Lone Wolf smiled slightly. "Well," he replied judiciously, "it depends on who's doin' the cussin'. The way you handed 'em out this morning, I considered them sorta authentic."

Uncle Mike chuckled, despite his evident depression.

"I don't mean perzactly that sort," he elaborated, "but the kind a feller puts onto somethin' he don't want anybody else to bother. Pertickler a feller what knows he's gonna die mighty soon."

Hatfield regarded him with greater gravity than before.

"Well," he said, "I consider there's this much to it — if folks know about the curse, it may affect them. I reckon most everybody is a mite superstitious, some more'n others. If folks get to thinking too much about such things, it turns into just another form of worrying, and worry allus has an effect, usually bad. Does that answer yore question?"

Uncle Mike nodded slowly. "Sorta," he admitted. "I don't figure I ever been over superstitious, but of late I've sorta had a leanin' that way. Fust I've got somethin' to show you, then I'll talk some more."

Shaw crossed to a ponderous iron safe, twirled the combination knob, swung back the massive door. Then he unlocked an inner compartment and rummaged among some papers. Finally he drew forth a yellowed bit of linen upon which was written something in rust-colored, crooked letters.

"You read Spanish?" he asked with a sharp look.

Hatfield nodded.

"Take a glim at this, then," said Uncle Mike. "Here, I'll turn up the lamp so's you kin see to make it out."

With curiosity which quickened to intense interest, Hatfield deciphered the rusty characters that spelled out the quaint Spanish of an earlier day.

I Fernando de Castro, in the tenth month of the *1810*-th year from man's salvation, am dying here where the last rays of sunlight reflected from the Devil's Finger fall upon my resting place and upon my lost mine, sealed by the dark men of the mountains who have slain my followers and wounded me to death. I am rich! Rich beyond my wildest dreams! But to what avail! The treasure is there — there where the red ray falls. It is mine!

I have paid for it with the substance of my soul! For it I murdered Enrique de Leon, my friend, to whom the King — may him God and the saints preserve — granted these lands. That deed haunts me and causes me much disquiet in my secret heart. For the others I do not care, for those who died toiling in the black dark. They are naught, those dark ones, although Father Juan, the priest, avowed that they have souls and in the after life may stand as high as the best blood of Castile.

That I believe not. There will be too many Dons and other gentlemen in Heaven who know how such things should be managed. But Enrique de Leon haunts me — he who was my friend. And because of this, my sin, I make penitence and send to the good Father Miguel Hidalgo of Guanajuato this message and with it that which tells the location of the treasure and the mine. I have one servitor left, he who hid me, wounded, from the wrath of the dark men of the mountains. He is small of wit but powerful of body.

Perhaps he can win through to the good priest with this my offering to Holy Church, whereupon prayers may be offered up for my soul. But I misdoubt me. To those who sit at the table of Death comes vision. Aye, I fear me that through the years without end the wealth shall lie hidden and the mine will remain indeed *La Mina Escondida.* If so, may a murderer's curse lie upon him who rolls away the stone!

Hatfield looked up from the strange document, to find old Mike Shaw's eyes fixed upon him.

"And," said old Mike heavily, "I was the feller who 'rolled away the stone'!"

Chapter 15
The Avalanche

For some minutes there was silence. Then old Mike spoke again.

"Yeah, I found it," he said in emotionless tones. "I got hold of this thing from a iggerent old Mexican I helped outa trouble. He give it to me jest 'fore he cashed in, and I figgered out the hidden ketch in it. It's almighty plain oncet you git onto it."

"How's that?" Hatfield asked.

Old Mike placed a horny finger on the words "Devil's Finger."

"That's it," he explained. "For years there's been the story goin' round that a old Spanish mine was hidden hereabouts and lotsa folks tried to locate it. I allus figgered it was jest another one of them yarns until I got hold of this thing. I knowed the country hereabouts, and I'd heerd tell of the Devil's Finger.

"That's what that big jut of rock up top the slope here is called. Well, when the sun is jest goin' down, late in the fall, it reflects from the side of the rock — it's granite polished by sand and wind — and the light falls down the slope here after the sun 'pears to have set. It's jest a narrer beam of light, and it only shows toward the end of the year.

"I was scratchin' round here last October and seed it, and all of a sudden the meanin' of them words come to me. I follered the beam up the slope, found where the rock and earth was all heaped up sorta onnachel-like under the brush, and uncovered *La Escondida*.

"But that ol' jigger musta been sorta loco jest before he died," Shaw added. "There isn't no treasure here like he talked about. A good claim, yes. I'm gettin' moderately well off from it, but that's all. Reckon he sorta sized it too high. Funny the priests never come lookin' for it."

"I don't figger that's over hard to explain," Hatfield put in. "That half-witted servant he speaks of was told to go to Father Miguel Hidalgo in Guanajuato, and that was in October of 1810. Well, Miguel Hidalgo y Costilla of Guanajuato, a priest, was the leader of the first real Mexican revolution, when all this section was the province of New Spain. He was captured and executed in 1811, the very next year.

"So of course the servant of old de Castro never got to him. Chances are he hung onto the writing — superstitious about it, no doubt, and it was handed down through his family. But what about the curse?"

"Well," said Uncle Mike heavily, "it was right after I opened up Escondida that things started happenin' in this district. There's folks what say that the Injuns in the mountains down below the border know their ancestors killed the Spaniards and closed the mine 'cause of the way the Spaniards made slaves of them and made 'em work theirselves to death in the mine.

"They say that the Injuns are mad 'cause the mine was opened agin and aim to run everybody outa the district and close it agin so's nobody will ever find it. That's one of the reasons I decided to start that new works over near the trail. I figgered that might cause 'em to ease up a mite."

"And you calc'late opening the mine is the reason for such a thing as the killing of Bruce Ralston and Sheriff Dobson?" Hatfield asked incredulously.

"Dunno," admitted Shaw, "but there's this about it. When I opened up I needed money to develop, so I took in three pardners with me. I hung onto more'n half the stock and have the say about everythin'. But them fellers put money into the thing, and everybody knows it."

"Well?"

"Well, one of them fellers was Bruce Ralston; another was Clate Dobson."

"And the third?"

"The third, he ain't dead yet. The third is young Joe Hayes."

Before he left the office, Hatfield agreed to install the hydraulic machinery for Shaw and start it operating.

"You hustle right over to Welch, the railroad town, tomorrer," directed old Mike. "They got a telegraph there and you can send in the order for the machinery by wire. You can ride it faster than the stage makes it. The inquest? Doc McChesney, the coroner, rode out to the head of the valley to tend a feller who got snakebit; won't be no inquest for a coupla days."

Hatfield started at daybreak and rode the forty-odd miles to the railroad town. He put in some busy hours at the telegraph office and satisfactorily arranged for the immediate shipment of the hydraulic mining machinery. That night, also, Captain McDowell at Ranger headquarters received a laconic unsigned telegram which read:

HAVING A REAL NICE TIME!

150

"Good gosh!" Captain Bill rumbled grimly, "I didn't figger things was that bad over there!"

It was late in the day when Hatfield concluded his transactions, so he spent the night at Welch. Early morning found him on the home trail. He was a little less than halfway to Coma when he turned aside from the Chisos Trail and entered the narrow mouth of a gloomy canyon that at first trended due south but later veered until it paralleled the Chisos Trail which clung to the mountainside far above.

The canyon floor was choked with growth, littered with boulders. The south wall was a great slope of shale and boulders and slide-scarred earth which swelled upward at a steep angle to the base of a series of battlemented cliffs that formed the serrated crests of the Phantoms.

"Must be a bad section in winter or early spring," Hatfield mused, eyeing the seamed and gashed slope. "Those gulches mean slides during freezing and melting times. Notion a gun shot or even a loud word would be enough to start those rocks rolling at times."

Mile after mile he made his way up the canyon, his keen eyes missing nothing. To all appearances the gloomy gorge was deserted and always had been, but from time to time Hatfield experienced an eerie feeling that he was being stalked by a creature or creatures invisible to the eye.

Strain his ears as he would, he could catch no sound of horses' irons on the rocks or the rattle of a misplaced stone. Still the feeling persisted, and it seemed to him, too, that Goldy was more nervous than was his wont, pricking his ears, rolling his dark eyes and manifesting uneasiness in various ways.

To men who ride throughout the years with deadly danger as a stirrup companion there comes a sixth sense that warns of menace when, apparently, none is present. Hatfield neither saw nor heard anything to substantiate the feeling, but nevertheless it persisted and the voiceless monitor deep in his brain persistently clamored for attention.

So while apparently he rode carelessly, lounging in the saddle, idling along through the growth, in reality every sense was at hairtrigger alertness.

Gloomier grew the canyon, as the cliffs on his right towered farther into the sky and their ragged breasts overhung the gorge floor. The slope on the left remained much the same save for an increase of the clusters of huge weather-rounded boulders that sprinkled the earth and shale.

Ahead, swelling from the canyon floor, appeared a tall knoll with sides practically free of growth. Hatfield absently noted that the side fronting the lower canyon was an almost perpendicular cliff while up canyon it was a steep rise that flowed upward to the rounded crest.

"Peculiar formation," he mused, "almost like the salt domes of the oil country. Looks almost like it had been thrown up by human hands, something like the burial pyramids of the Aztecs covered with earth and grass."

He dismissed the mound from his thoughts upon passing it, however, and concentrated on that which had brought him into the canyon in the first place.

"That chimney rock cliff over there had oughta be just about opposite where the horse went over," he decided, "if I didn't mistake the spot on the way to Welch yesterday. There's the overhang that marks the trail up above. Now let's see, four, five hundred yards farther oughta about make it. Shore is shadowy down here since the canyon narrowed just t'other side of that mound."

Hatfield rode on, pushed through a final straggle of brush and abruptly pulled up.

Directly before him lay the carcass of the unfortunate horse that had plunged over the lip of the trail on the night of his arrival.

"Just as I figgered, a black," he muttered. "Gosh, he's squashed like a stepped-on frog! And," he added quietly, his green eyes narrowing and becoming coldly gray, "someone got here before I did!"

That was self-evident. The horse Hatfield saw plunge over the lip of the cliff trail had worn saddle and bridle. The mangled body before him bore neither. And a second glance showed a ragged wound where the brand had been cut away.

"Just as I had it figgered out," Hatfield growled. "That poor devil, Bruce Ralston, managed somehow to give the hellions the slip while he still had some life left in his body. He grabbed a gun off one of 'em and forked a horse what also belonged to one of the gang. Made his getaway, but was plugged doing it. Rode till he fell outa the hull. Scared the cayuse when he dropped and it run away. Wonder why they didn't follow him?

"Perhaps they did, and he gave them the slip. Perhaps they heard his gun when he throwed down on me and figgered that meant somebody was coming and didn't care to risk meeting anybody, pertickler when they had no way of knowing how many somebodies it might be.

"Which means, if I'm guessing right in this, that whoever they are, they shore don't wanta be spotted. That hardly ties up with the Indian theory. This critter's gear and brand musta meant something too, if they took the trouble to sneak up here and remove both. Question is, how did they know he went over here? They coulda trailed the getaway and found Ralston's body, but there wasn't a thing to show the horse went over the cliff nearly half a mile farther on.

"Nope, that's out. My guess is that they didn't know about it until Sheriff Dobson brought Ralston's body to town. I calc'late the jigger what cashed in Ralston is the one who hightailed here to remove evidence that would tie him up with the killing of Ralston. Shore wish I knew who all Sheriff Dobson talked to other than the men I met in his office, if anybody else. Mebbe Walt Wagner will know."

Dismounting, Hatfield went over every inch of ground near the dead horse. Suddenly he voiced a low exclamation. Beside a bush, where the earth was soft and moist, he found a footprint.

"And no Indian moccasin ever made that track," he muttered, eyeing the deep and

155

clean-cut indentation of a high, narrow boot heel.

"Cowboy boot," he added, "about average size. No pertickler nail pattern or anything to make it out from any other one. And this *is* a moccasin print!"

Squatting on his heels, Hatfield examined a second track discovered near the first, shaking his head over the broad loose scuffing so unlike the mark made by the boot. Carefully he quartered the ground and came to the conclusion that two men had been active around the body of the horse.

"And from all appearances, an Indian and a white man," he decided, "or at least one of them wore boots and the other moccasins."

Hatfield continued his examination, farther down canyon, and unearthed indubitable evidence of the recent presence of two horses.

"Beginning to tie up," he declared. "One horse shod with regulation irons, t'other one on bare hoofs. *That* says white man and Indian, all right."

Exhaustive search discovered nothing further of interest and Hatfield mounted and rode slowly back down the canyon, more watchful than before. For more and more urgent was the clamor of that unheard voice crying of pressing hidden danger.

Boom!

The sound was like to the discharge of a great gun. It snapped Hatfield's head back, caused Goldy to snort and shy. It was instantly followed by a crackling rattle as of volleying rifle fire.

For a tense moment the Lone Wolf was utterly at a loss to account for the unusual sounds. Then, as his eye ran over the scene, he saw turbulent movement far up the rugged slope to his right. For a bewildered instant he stared, then with a rush came understanding. The slope was roaring downward toward the canyon floor in a mighty avalanche!

Even as Hatfield stared, the advance of the slide struck the canyon floor with a low, thudding thunder. Huge boulders came bounding toward him, flattening the growth, smashing everything in their path to powder. And this was only the beginning. Behind these deadly outriders, with a slow serpentine movement, came the body of the avalanche.

"On, Goldy!" Hatfield roared.

The great sorrel fled down the canyon with death crashing at his heels. Almost instantly Hatfield realized that the race was lost before it was begun. For fully a mile ahead the entire slope was now in motion, a mighty mass of earth and stone that would sweep across the canyon floor like the Atlantic over a lost continent.

But on fled the great golden horse, gallantly running his losing race with death. Eyes rolling, mane tossing, nostrils flaring red, he poured his long body over the ground. His flying irons crashed showers of sparks from the stones, foam from gaping jaws flecking his glorious golden coat.

Hatfield steadied him, upheld him, encouraging him to greater efforts with voice and hand. And ever the huge boulders thundered past, missing them by inches, by the breadth of a hair, while smaller stones screamed overhead and crashed against the canyon wall with the force of shots fired from a battleship's guns.

A hurricane of displaced air howled and under all, a base for the wild turmoil, was a horrible crunching and grinding, the most sickening sound Hatfield had ever listened to.

In a level wall, a score of feet and more high, the avalanche came rolling and thundering across the canyon floor. High above the doomed horse and his rider curved the ragged tossing crest, with mighty masses of stone and earth rushing down the concave surface like wreckage on the breast of a wave.

CHAPTER 16
"KILL YOU IF WE CAN!"

With the roaring destruction less than a hundred yards away, Hatfield suddenly saw a brown swelling mass directly ahead. He let out a yell of renewed hope which spurred the straining horse to a last frenzied effort.

With the first broken masses of the avalanche crashing at his very heels, Goldy's irons hit the slope of the high knoll which swelled from the canyon floor. Up he went, clawing like a cat at the steep rise, gasping, sobbing, striving to distance that awful terror which boomed and thundered in his ears.

The mighty buttress of stone shook and trembled from the force of the blow as the avalanche struck. Up the slope foamed a welter of earth and rock. Over it screeched the flying boulders. More than halfway to the very crest of the tall hill the frothing rubble piled and folded, sending gushing forth billows of dust and showers of rock splinters.

The broadly foundationed knoll rocked and swayed, as if it would be torn bodily from the granite upon which it was based. It shuddered like a living thing in pain as giant boulders crashed against its sides, tearing away tons of stone which went flying across the narrow canyon to burst in meteor fragments against the adamantine cliffs.

Gradually the turmoil lessened, ceased. A vast cloud of dust swirled and eddied through the canyon. This too at length settled. The air cleared, the sunshine filtered through and the tender blue of the sky arch gazed downward at the destruction wrought.

For full a mile and a half the slope was ripped and scarred, denuded of every vestige of growth, scoured clean of boulders and loose rock. Only the glistening naked stone or the raw wound of fresh earth was visible. The canyon floor was buried many feet deep with a tossed and swaled sea of marl.

Hatfield stared, shaking his head, his quick gaze taking in the whole scene at a glance that traveled upward toward the distant line of cliffs which surmounted the slope.

"Now how in blazes did that thing get started?" he muttered. "Seemed to me the first thing I heard was a sound like that of an explosion. Was that a big mass of stone breaking loose from a cliff to start the mass sliding, or was it something else? I wonder if —"

With a lithe movement of bewildering speed he swayed sideways, hurling himself out of the saddle. He struck the earth on hands and knees and was erect in a catlike leap, hand reaching for the butt of the heavy Winchester snugged in the saddle boot.

Cr-rr-rack! Whe-e-e-e! Spat!

Something screeched and crackled through the space his body had occupied the instant before, caromed off a jut of stone and slammed against the cliff.

Hatfield had heard that splitting, crackling sound before, and once heard it is never forgotten — the passage of a high-power rifle bullet fearfully close. Only his instant reaction to a slight flicker of movement and a winking gleam where the denuded slope joined the base of the distant cliffs had saved him.

"Sunlight slanting on the hellion's rifle barrel!" Hatfield muttered as his own saddle gun lined sights across Goldy's withers.

Hatfield's green eyes, cold and deadly as the steel of the Winchester itself, glanced along the length of the barrel as a second slug whined past. Then the Winchester spoke, once, twice, a third time. Puffs of dust along the base of the cliff told where the bullets struck.

The Lone Wolf worked the ejection lever in a spinning blur of movement, shifted the black muzzle the merest trifle, squeezed the trigger a fourth time.

Smoke wisped from the rifle. The echoes slammed back and forth between the cliff. Hatfield lowered his gun and stood staring at the black dot that had suddenly straightened, wavered an instant and then pitched forward. It hit the slope, slid, rolled, spun downward faster and faster, gathering to itself an increment of earth and bits of shale.

But the slope had been swept too clean for a second avalanche to result. The body reached the canyon floor in a cloud of dust and lay without sound or movement.

Hatfield did not spare it a glance. His whole attention was centered on the ominous shadow at the base of the distant cliffs. Back and forth his hawk glance traveled, until he had convinced himself that the drygulcher had no companion holed up somewhere and awaiting an opportunity to crack down.

"Playing a lone hand, I reckon," Hatfield muttered. "Okay, Goldy, let's see if we can shuffle over there and take a look at what's left of that hellion. Reckon *he* was responsible for you running yore legs down to yore knee caps. Thanks, feller — if it hadn't been for you I'd be buried so deep they'd hafta call out the reserves to dig me out in time for the Judgment!"

It was a hard flounder across the jumble of raw earth and littered stone, but they made it. Hatfield knelt beside the battered thing that had once been a man. With narrowing lids he noted the lank black hair falling in a straight bang over the swarthy forehead, the beady eyes, the high cheekbones. The face was very dark, almost black.

"Yaqui, judging from all appearances," he muttered. "Yaqui rig, too."

Abruptly Hatfield bent lower, peering at the lank hair. With a tentative finger he raised a hanging lock, brushed it away from the forehead, let it fall back again.

"Well, I'll be damned!" he growled.

He bent a long look at the dark face, then turned his attention to the dead man's accouterments.

The broad cartridge bandolier caught his eye. He fingered the empty loops. The fellow's pistol belt was full, but there weren't half a dozen rifle shells left.

"Musta done a heap of shooting of late," Hatfield grunted. Then his eyes blazed with excitement. "Gosh, no!" he exclaimed. "That *was* an explosion I heard just before the avalanche started. This hellion emptied the powder from his rifle cartridges and set off a charge under a big boulder or a loose section of the cliff, knowing it would set the whole slope to sliding and catch me before I could get out.

"Smart! Wouldn'ta left a trace of me or Goldy either. Damned smart! Too smart for a Yaqui! He didn't figger on that knoll, but who would! I didn't either, until it was right in front of me. He could see me riding, of course, before the dust got too thick, and I reckon he was some flabbergasted to see me sittin' up top there after it cleared. Took a chance and lined sights on me.

"Mighty nigh got by with that, too. That little flicker of sun on his rifle barrel gave him away. Hmmm! Looks like somebody's getting sorta worried, and sorta anxious to blot my brand. I was right about the way I felt all day. Somebody *was* following me — been following me ever since I left town.

"When I turned into this canyon he figgered I was shore up to no good. Perhaps figgered me for knowing more'n I did. Well, *now* mebbe I know a lot more than they figger me to know!"

A careful search of the body revealed

nothing of interest. Hatfield left it where it lay and began the difficult journey down the canyon. Both he and Goldy were heartily sick of the job by the time they reached the mouth. But nevertheless Hatfield was elated; he had learned something that he considered gravely important.

"Hair!" he mused as they turned into the Chisos Trail. "A hair rope is strong enough to stop and hold a tough steer. Funny if just a few scattered hairs prove to be enough to hang a gent!"

The day was far advanced and purple shadows were flowing up the canyon walls as the Lone Wolf rode the gloomy reaches under the overhang of the cliffs. As the Chisos Trail wound over the withers of a great ridge, a golden autumn moon soared up from behind the eastern crags, paled to silver and washed the naked pinnacles with ashen light. The purple shadows became ebon and the twisted forms of chimney rock and spire were grotesque and weird in the deceptive radiance and seemed charged with malevolent life.

A solemn hush brooded over the lonely mountains and Goldy's irons rang dully, the clean-cut edge of the sound furred and flattened by the swathing cloak of the silence. And then, born of the misty moonlight, the glowering stone and the shadows, there came a sibilant whispering that swelled to an ominous mutter and growl.

"We will kill you! We will kill you if we can!" said the drums to the east.

"We will kill you! We will kill you!" answered the drums to the west.

And then in sinister muttering chorus: "We will kill you! We will kill you! We will kill you if we can!"

CHAPTER 17
FROM THE DARK

In the office of the Escondida Mine in Coma a bitter argument was in progress. Old Mike Shaw was there, and Walt Wagner, the fat deputy sheriff, wetting his lips with the tip of a nervous tongue. There too was handsome, dark Henry Lyons, owner of the Arrow ranch, and sullen young Joe Hayes. Big old Train Beverly, owner of the XT, made a substantial balance at the foot of the long table.

"I tell you, Uncle Mike, I don't like it," Hayes was declaring. "Here a danged range tramp ambles into town and 'cause he happens to have a horse strong enough to haul a stick of wood off top of a coupla rock busters, you go 'haid and practically put him in charge of the mine. I say it's plumb damphoolishness. 'Member, I've got some money tied up in this business."

"You wanta sell out?" Uncle Mike countered quick as a hair trigger. "I'm ready to buy, if you do."

Hayes screwed up his good looking but sullen face into an obstinate knot.

"Nope, I don't," he declared, "but I want a run for my money, that's all."

"You'll git it," creaked old Mike. "I tell you, all you fellers, this jigger Hatfield knows his business. The way he talked about this hydraulic stuff convinced me right off. I may not be plumb up on these newfangled methods, but I do know the minin' business, and Hatfield mighty quick showed me he'd forgot more about geology and the mechanical end of minin' than I ever knowed. I wouldn't be s'prised if he turned out to be one of them engineer fellers wanderin' around on a prospectin' jaunt of his own."

Henry Lyons bent an inscrutable glance upon the speaker and tapped his long, blue-shaven chin with a supple forefinger.

Young Joe flushed darkly. "Somethin' like that's jest what I'm scairt of!" he spat. "I'm scairt that jigger is too all-fired smart, and when we wake up to everything he's done we'll find ourselves hangin' onto the muddy end of the stick."

"Feller with eyes like his'n is liable to be anythin'," grumbled Walt Wagner in substantiation. "My gosh! when he looked at me t'other night over them gunsights, I felt like I was gonna ooze away into a grease spot."

"You looked it," Hayes agreed contemptuously. "I figger you sweated off about five pounds while he was holdin' the irons on us."

"I didn't see you do no highfalutin' stunts!" Wagner fired back at him. "I thought you was gonna squeeze yore gun stock into clabber, the way you hung onto it when he made you look like a terrapin tryin' to pull a frawg outa a hole. That jigger could roll and light a cigaroot after you reached and still beat you to clearin' leather!"

"Don't you think this is all rather outa order?" Henry Lyons remarked in acid tones. "We all know Walt is too damn fat, and we likewise know Joe paws for his gun like a cub bear reaching for a stick. What we came here to discuss is the disposal of Ralston's and Dobson's shares in the Escondida. I can't figger how we got onto this new hand Uncle Mike hired."

"You're right, Lyons," Hayes growled agreement. "I reckon the feller jest sorta rubbed me the wrong way. I felt purty bad over pore ol' Bruce. After all, he was my fust cousin and sorta raised me. Reckon I'm jest nacherly a mite tetchy."

"Speakin' of that," broke in Uncle Mike

Shaw, "I don't reckon there'll be any argument as to who'll fall heir to Ralston's share in the mine. I calc'late you to be the only relative he had on earth, so far as anybody ever heerd tell of, Joe. Isn't that right?"

"I reckon so," Hayes agreed, adding reluctantly, "but I don't feel jest right about takin' over his ownin's. Mebbe Bruce mighta wanted somebody else to have 'em."

"I don't figger that," said old Train Beverly. "Clate Dobson was the only close friend Bruce had, and Clate's gone, too. The courts will be plumb sartain to hand the Bowtie and everything else over to you, Joe, and you can't very well do anythin' but accept 'em.

"But as to pore ol' Clate's holdin's, I don't know. He didn't have nobody, I reckon. If he owed any debts the shares is like to be sold to satisfy 'em. Anyhow, Uncle Mike owns controllin' interest, and he's the one what'll have the say as to how Escondida is run."

"I still figger we ought to keep on with the original mine," grumbled Hayes, argumentative to the last. "I don't go for these newfangled contraptions. We —"

Abruptly he paused, a queer look on his face, a glow in his deep-set eyes. Silence blanketed the room. Henry Lyons stared

171

inscrutably out the open window, only a ripple of muscle along the angle of his jaw hinting at stress or emotion. The others sat tense and rigid, listening.

And through the open window came a whisper, a mutter, a vibrating beat. The mine building squatted on the lip of the slope some distance above the town, and the garrulous rumble of activity from the streets below was muted to a mere murmur.

All about was moon-drenched stillness, with the black tower of the Phantoms swelling toward the star-flecked sky. From far up the dark slope came the sound, persistent, penetrating. A monotonous beat that swelled and ebbed, swelled and ebbed — the harsh rasp of horny fingers drawn across taut hide.

"We will kill you! We will kill you! We will kill you if we can!"

Joe Hayes broke the tense silence in the room. "They sound mad-like, snarlin'," he muttered. He glanced at the drawn faces of his companions.

"Gents," he said, his voice dry with strain, "gents, I betcha there's a body layin' back in the hills somewhere."

The men glanced from one to another. "That feller Hatfield," mouthed old Train Beverly. "He's comin' through the hills tonight, ain't he, Mike?"

172

"Uh-huh," Shaw replied in flat tones. "Uh-huh, and he'd oughta been here hours ago."

Young Joe Hayes stared, the strained expression of his features intensified. Henry Lyons relaxed in his chair. And through the ash of the moonlight filtered the ominous threat.

"We will kill you if we can. We will kill you if we can!"

The sinister mutter died away, ceased. The occupants of the room stirred, shifted their positions. Joe Hayes stood up.

"I'm moseyin' down into town to git me a drink," he announced. "Comin' along, Walt?"

The fat deputy nodded agreement. Henry Lyons left his chair, stared out the window a moment.

"We didn't settle much of anything," he remarked, "but I reckon it'll keep. Good night, Mike."

Lyons left the room and a moment later Train Beverly also took his departure. Old Mike remained seated at the table, bending over a scrawl of figures. His back was to the open window which, as the moon climbed higher, was a black rectangle of shadow.

Absorbed in his work, Shaw did not hear the stealthy, almost imperceptible scratch of feet on the ground outside the window. He did not see the solider shadow that loomed in the black rectangle, nor the glint of eyes through mask holes under a low-drawn hat brim.

For a long moment the glowing eyes fixed on the curved back of the old man. Then a hand appeared — a hand that gripped a short-barreled gun. The black barrel rested on the window ledge, steadied, lined with a spot between poor old Mike's scrawny shoulder blades. For a tense instant the killer stood poised, outlined hard and clear against the light within. Then the room rocked to a heavy report.

CHAPTER 18
THE STORY OF PENELOSA

It seemed to Jim Hatfield that the drum-beats which followed him across the withers of the great ridge were different from those he heard the night Bruce Ralston was murdered. Then they were exultant, triumphant, a swelling rattle and boom that chanted of victory.

Tonight they were sullen, baffled, snarling of frustration and rasping vindictive threat. Their beat followed him down the moon-washed trail, pacing his advance, never drawing nearer, but never retreating. They seemed to hold, too, a note of expectancy; they were impatient, but they were waiting, sure of the ultimate result.

Next to the cliff wall was black shadow, and Hatfield kept his stirrup rasping against the rock. Never once did he venture into the pale light that lipped the crumbly edge and crawled ghost-like across the dusty surface. And ever and anon his green eyes swept the trail ahead, and the sinister spires and crags on the far side of the great gorge.

"They're over there somewhere," Hatfield growled. "Over there among the rocks. They know I'm riding here and they're letting me know they know it. But it's too damn far to line sights on me here in the shadow. They know that, too, and they also know that steady beat is almighty hard on the nerves. Feller is apt to get panicky as it keeps on and on. Get panicky and make a dash for it, slide out into the moonlight, and be all set to get a slug through him.

"A good saddle gun will carry 'crost the gorge all right, and carry to what a bead's drawn on, too. Thousand yards, mebbe a little more; but a Winchester like I'm packing is sighted for that and then some. Would be mighty nice shooting, and it couldn't be done by the kinda irons Indians usually carry. Nor," he added cryptically, "by the kinda shooting Indians usually do."

On and on he rode, alert, watchful, until the gorge abruptly ended and the trail dipped over the crest and slid downward toward where the distant lights of Coma glowed like earthbound stars. And as the great sorrel quickened his pace and Hatfield breathed a sigh of relief, from amid the spires and pinnacles, black against the moonlight, the hidden drums snarled and cursed with baffled hate.

Hatfield cut across from the trail and approached the big stable from the rear. There were both front and rear doors and the paunchy little stable keeper who slept above the stalls had given him a key to the back door.

"Don't usually do this," he explained, "but Uncle Mike recommended you strong and that makes things sorta different." He added with a gulpy chuckle: "Reckon I'd done it anyhow, oncet I got a squint at that cayuse of yores. Feller with a hoss like that don't go liftin' crowbaits. He's got too good jedgment and taste."

Hatfield grinned at the left-handed compliment and accepted the key. Now he was glad of it, for it was late and the stable keeper might be hard to arouse.

With the swift efficiency of long years of practice, he cared for the sorrel and made him comfortable for the night. Then he locked the stable door again and cut across toward the gaunt loom of the Escondida building.

He was much later than he had expected his return to be, and he wished to allay any anxiety on the part of Uncle Mike Shaw. On silent feet he rounded the corner of the rambling structure and halted dead, every nerve strained to a quivering tension.

Directly ahead was a ray of light that poured from an open window. And clearly outlined against the light, a masked man leveled a gun across the window sill!

Hatfield instantly realized that the light came from Uncle Mike's office; and as instantly he acted. A blurring flicker of his right hand, a focusing stare of the green eyes and his Colt roared just as the drygulcher tensed to pull trigger.

Hatfield saw the short-barreled gun spin from the killer's hand, heard his yelp of surprise and pain. Then, blinded momentarily by the flash of his own gun, the Lone Wolf leaped forward, shaking his head to clear his eyes.

Three running strides he took, and he was hurled backward by a tremendous blow on his chest.

So violent was the impact that it spun Hatfield off his feet and sent him crashing to the ground. Gasping for breath, he saw flame gush out of the dark beside the window, heard the wail of a slug through the air over his prostrate form. He rolled sideways, sent three shots roaring toward the flash and rolled again.

But there was no answering blaze of

gunfire, only a swift whisper of running feet. Hatfield sent another slug whining in the direction of the sound, shifted position and listened. There was a last fading patter, then silence broken by the curses Uncle Mike Shaw was screeching through the open window.

Hatfield got painfully to his feet, feeling of the burning welt along his ribs.

"Didn't figger on there being a wire fence built along here," he grunted. "But mebbe it's a good thing I didn't. That hellion was almighty fast to get at his second iron and that little 'hello-good-bye' he sent in my direction came mighty close as it was. Mighta been wuss than close if I'd been standing up.

"All right, Shaw!" he shouted. "It's me — Hatfield. Don't go throwin' no lead out that window."

"What the blankety-blank-blank-blank is goin' on round here?" howled Uncle Mike. "Where'd this hawglaig with a busted butt plate come from? What's all the shootin' about?"

Hatfield climbed the triple strands of wire that hemmed in the building. He skirted the open window, out of which Uncle Mike was now leaning, gun in hand, and entered the office.

Shaw had his own gun in one hand, in the other he was holding a stubby-barreled iron with one butt plate missing. Unheeding the old man's yammer of questions, Hatfield took the damaged weapon from his hand and examined it.

"Uh-huh," he growled, "just as I figgered. This is the thing that killed Sheriff Dobson. See, it's a thirty-two-twenty, and," he added grimly, "it isn't the one I took off pore Ralston back there on the trail. This is the mate to that one, or I'm a heap mistook. That one went away with the hellion who was lining sights on you when I happened along."

In a few terse sentences he informed Uncle Mike of what he had seen upon rounding the corner, and described the subsequent happenings. Shaw drew a long breath.

"Thanks, son," he said quietly, but with deep feeling. "Now what all happened to you today? Why you so late gettin' back?"

Hatfield told him briefly, but omitting no important details. Shaw listened, his wrinkled old face drawn into stern lines. He nodded with satisfaction over the fate of the drygulcher who had started the avalanche, shook his head over the pursuing drums.

"They're out to git you, son," he declared.

"They figger you're hornin' into their game, whatever it is, and they don't like it." He hesitated, rasping his chin with a stubby forefinger.

"I don't like to say this," he remarked slowly, "don't like to say it on my own account, 'cause I figger you to be mighty valuable to me in more'n one way right now, but I figger it's to yore best interests for me to say it. I'm gonna give you a mite of advice — fork that big yaller hoss of yore's and ride, ride fast and far. Git plumb outa this section while you're in shape to git out. Them hellions is bad — they proved it more'n oncet — and they'll be after you wuss'n ever after this day's work. That's my advice, son."

"Thanks," Hatfield replied. "I reckon it's good advice, all right, and I'm much obliged to you for it."

"You're takin' it, then?" asked Shaw.

Hatfield smiled down at him from his great height, but it was a smile of the lips only. His green eyes were somber and cold as a winter storm cloud.

"Nope," he said evenly, "I'm not!"

Uncle Mike sighed. "I calc'lated as much," he admitted. "It's damphoolishness for you to hang on, with things like they are, but you're shore a almighty nice fool!"

Hatfield grinned slightly, and changed the subject.

"They're gonna rush the machinery. We were lucky. A stock had been assembled at their Texas headquarters for shipment into Mexico, but the deal down there is hanging fire and they say we can have it. It was being packed for shipment to us before I finished wiring. We should have it on hand in a few days."

"Fine!" exclaimed Uncle Mike, adding pessimistically, "pervidin' any of us is alive to handle it when it gits here. Things are shore gittin' bad in this section. Almost as bad as they was years and years ago, at the time of the Howard-Penelosa law suit and the killin's what sprouted outa that."

Hatfield looked his interest. "How was that?" he asked.

"It's a considerable yarn," said Uncle Mike, "but I reckon it's wuth listenin' to. It come about this way: you'll rec'lect that old writin' I showed you t'other night said somethin' about the King of Spain grantin' all the land in this section to a feller named Enrique de Leon?

"Well, that warn't no tanglewood tale — that actually happened, all right. It's history. That feller Enrique de Leon got killed somehow — jest how doesn't appear to be quite clear, from the records. But I reckon old de Castro did him in somehow, as he confessed in his writin'.

"Anyhow, de Leon was cashed in, but he left relatives, heirs to his property. Them relatives, some of 'em at any rate, were in Mexico at the time. When de Leon didn't come back, his grandson, a feller by the name of Ramon Penelosa, come up here and took charge of Mescalero Valley, built him a ranch house, brought in cattle, lived here for years. Then —"

Sitting under the guttering lamp, with the window shutters closed against a chance return of the mysterious drygulcher, Jim Hatfield listened with intense interest to a stirring story of blood and greed and hatred and revenge of a bygone day.

CHAPTER 19
BLOOD OF SPAIN

A proud man was Don Ramon Penelosa. In his veins ran the blood of kings of Aragon and of Moorish princes. His grandfather, the father of his stately mother, had been Don Enrique de Leon, friend and favorite of the Spanish king, the most powerful ruler of his day. In gratitude for the deeds of that sturdy soldier, Don Enrique, the king had given to him a great grant of land in the province of New Spain. Don Enrique had journeyed to the wild new land in search of added fame and fortune, and had found — a grave!

Of this Don Ramon was thinking as he sat on the cool veranda of his spacious hacienda and gazed south by east toward where, misty with distance, the dark bulk of the Phantoms reared against the Texas sky. Don Ramon's gaze rested, and held, upon a mighty spire of stone that shot upward from the broken crest of the most westerly slope.

It was a peculiar appearing formation, that grim upward fling of naked stone. Mighty at the base, it tapered slightly, with a gnarled swelling midway its length, and from that swelling to its blunted tip, it bent inward slightly, for all the world like a gigantic beckoning finger. The Devil's Finger, the first men of Spain had named the great shaft of stone. To this day men furtively crossed themselves when they gazed upon the ominous, beckoning finger of dark rock.

The winds and rains of countless ages had polished the stone to a mirror-like smoothness, and mirror-like it reflected the rays of the sun, concentrating and casting them afar in a dazzling beam that blinded the eye like the flash from a beacon light. The low-lying sun beat squarely on the lofty tip at the moment, and the reddish ray shot lance-like over Don Ramon's hacienda toward the unseen crests of the Cienagos beyond the mouth of the Mescalero Valley.

Don Ramon studied the ray, his shrewd black eyes narrowing with speculation, his lips smiling the smile of one who anticipates a pleasing event. Don Ramon was thinking of a legend that was more than a legend, a story that had come down to him from his grandfather's time. He turned to his young son, little more than a boy, who sat on the far side of the table. With a supple finger he tapped a parchment that lay on the table, a parchment covered with intricate mathematical calculations.

"Success, my son!" he exulted in cultured Spanish. "The problem is at last solved. Soon the time will be at hand and we will acquire the wealth secreted by your illustrious ancestor who met so untimely a death. Here upon the parchment is the answer — see, I have worked it out to the last detail."

The boy stared at the figures, but vaguely comprehending their significance, and not in the least understanding the intricate processes by which the solution had been arrived at.

"Si," continued Don Ramon, "it is here, but only my eye can read aright the meaning. Here is the key to wealth, my son, the wealth which shall send you across the waters to study in the great university of medicine and acquire the knowledge which will so benefit our people. Here, my son, into your care I give the parchment. Guard it until the time has come."

The boy took the paper, albeit reluctantly.

"But, Father," he protested, "I would rather stay with you than go across the waters. Cannot I study in our own land of *Mejico?*"

Don Ramon smiled tolerantly, but replied with the despotic assurance of the teachings of an older land and an earlier day.

"Only in the land of your fathers can you acquire the greatest of knowledge," he replied with finality. "Peace! All is decided."

The boy bowed his head obediently and left his father's presence, bearing with him the parchment. Don Ramon glanced up at the last gleam of the fiery ray and gave himself over to pleasant speculation.

Don Ramon was again sitting on his veranda the following afternoon when two men rode up, dismounted and approached the *casa*. Don Ramon arose courteously to receive them. One he recognized as the sheriff of the county, a shifty-eyed individual with a scrawny mustache drooping over a weak mouth. He was not a native Texan, but a dubious member of the rapacious followers of the devastation of war. He had achieved office by shifty political intrigue, as had altogether too many officials of the Texas of those dark times.

The other man was a stranger to Don Ramon. He was big-bodied, heavy-jowled, with a square chin, a merciless tight mouth, and a truculent eye. His glance was one of disdain as it rested on the dignified Mexican, and it was plain to see that he had nothing but contempt for the courtly but inefficient sons of the land of *mañana.*

The pair mounted the steps and the sheriff drew a folded paper from his pocket. He cleared his throat and tried to meet the grandee's inquiring gaze with a truculent swagger.

"Don Ramon," he announced, "you done lost the suit brought against you. The judge has ruled you're on this land unlawful and I got a court order here orderin' you to vacate."

Ramon Penelosa stared, his face darkening with anger. "But, *señor,*" he replied, albeit quickly, "I do not understand. This land was granted my ancestor by the then King of Spain. Such grants have before now been recognized by the courts of this land."

The sheriff grunted in his throat. "The King of Spain ain't no great shakes in Texas these days," he growled, "and he didn't have no business grantin' Texas land to nobody. This grant ain't recognized by the court, and the court's tellin' you to git out, pronto, and make room for Mr. Howard, here, who's filed all proper and has got a grant from the state capital."

Don Ramon stood lance straight and held the pair with his burning glance. Howard's cold gaze did not waver, but the sheriff shifted uneasily.

"I will appeal," the *hidalgo* declared. "I refuse to recognize as final the decree of Judge Dowley, whom I know to be a creature of imported politicians, such as you yourself are. There are honest men in Texas, no matter what their blood or birth. I will appeal."

John Howard spoke for the first time. "You ain't got no grounds for appeal," he stated harshly. "This thing is settled all proper and legal, and there ain't no appeal, pertickler from this."

His hand flashed down as he spoke and came up holding a heavy gun. Don Ramon did not move, nor was there need.

From the doorway behind him crashed a stunning report. With a curse Howard reeled back, clawing at his right arm, from which blood spouted. The sheriff shot both hands high into the air.

Still Don Ramon did not move, nor did his expression alter.

"*Gracias,* Pedro," he said over his shoulder, then to Howard:

"You see I have servitors who are loyal and upon whom I can rely for protection from the lawless. Let this be a lesson to you. Go, now, and do not come back. I will appeal this ruling in the prescribed manner and justice will be done." He spoke again over his shoulder.

"Pedro, come forth."

The man who stepped from the doorway held a cocked rifle in his hands. His lean, craggy face was swarthy almost to blackness. He wore his lank black hair cut in a square bang that fell over his low forehead. His beady black eyes stared at Howard with pleasurable anticipation.

"Pedro," said Don Ramon, "ride after these men and see that they leave my lands. That is all. *Adios, Señores.*"

The swarthy man gestured with his rifle.

John Howard had seen full-blood Yaqui Indians before, and he had also seen something of their work. White with anger and pain, his eyes blazing with baffled fury, he yet had sense enough not to hesitate or argue.

He followed the sheriff down the steps and clumsily mounted his horse, cherishing his bullet-punctured arm. One long look he bent upon the impassive *hidalgo,* then he rode away after the shivering sheriff, the grim *Indio* shepherding them, his eyes hungry for slaughter.

But John Howard was a hard man, and he had other hard men at his beck and call. Three nights later, just as the gray ghost of the dawn was stealing across the sky, Don Ramon Penelosa was awakened by a crash of rifle fire and a roaring of flames. He leaped from his bed as the front door of his casa was battered down. Through the window he could see his barns blazing and his servitors being shot down by unseen rifles as they rushed from their adobes. Flinging open the door of his bedroom, he confronted John Howard, one arm bandaged, a gun in his good hand.

Howard shot him through the mouth and he fell, gasping and writhing, blood gushing over the polished floor. There was a scream of agony and Don Ramon's young son rushed forward and knelt beside his dying father.

Don Ramon stared into his face with glazing eyes and tried to speak. But only a blood bubbling gabble of sound resulted. His tongue had been shot in two. He fell back and in another moment was dead. The boy glared up with wild, frightened eyes.

John Howard stepped forward a pace, grim, purposeful, his gun jutting forward. But before he could cover the boy a figure was before him. It was the old *señora,* the mother of Don Ramon. She fronted Howard, raised her shriveled arms and blighted him with her flashing eyes. Then she cursed him with a terrible curse, a curse to reach down through the ages with its dire threat of blood and death and agony and tears.

"Even as you have done unto this house may God do unto you and yours!" she finished. "May you die in blood and pain, and those who come after you. May this land run red with their blood until justice be done. I see it. I see it! With my old eyes I see it! May you and all that is yours droop and wither from this night on!"

John Howard, hard as he was, quailed before the frantic figure and the bitter, burning words. He stepped back, sheathing his gun, and gestured to the grim old woman and the cowering boy.

"Drive 'em out with the rest of the scum!" he growled. "No more killin'. Herd 'em over the border into Mexico. Get goin'!"

Old Mike Shaw's voice ceased, and Jim Hatfield came back to the present with a start. He stared at the mine owner.

"One grand yarn, all right," he agreed. "What happened after that?"

Old Mike shrugged. "Them was stern days," he replied, "and there was a lotta bad things done and got away with. Howard had that crooked sheriff from up Nawth in cahoots with him, and I heerd tell that ol'

Jedge Dowley was of similar stripe. Anyway, after drivin' what was left of Don Ramon's outfit, includin' the son and the old grandmother, down into Mexico, Howard cleaned out most of the other Mexicans in the valley, got the order of the lower court confirmed and his grant declared legal and took over Penelosa's spread.

"Things what happened was sorta hushed up, I reckon; but that feller Pedro, who was a Yaqui but eddicated in a mission, come outa the mess with a whole skin and passed on the story of what happened jest as I told it to you."

"Wonder what become of the boy?" Hatfield mused.

"Stayed down in *mañana* land, I reckon," Shaw replied. "Never nothin' heerd tell of him so far as I been able to ascertain. Reckon them figgers the old don worked out didn't mean nothin' to him, though I calc'late they showed how to find the Escondida Mine. Chances are he's been dead years. Be an old, old man now if he isn't. Them things happened a mighty long time back. Howard evidently never took no stock in the yarn. He didn't file on this hill section — jest down in the valley where there was good range, which was lucky for me and other prospectors."

"And what happened to Howard?"

"Him? Oh, he went and got hisself killed all proper in a poker game here in Coma. Died mighty onpleasant and painful, I understand, and took a long time to do it. Kept gabblin' about the cuss the old *señora* put on him. His daughter inherited the Bowtie — that's what he named Penelosa's spread. She married Bruce Ralston.

"They didn't have no kids, and when she died, the spread come down to Bruce. Now he's dead and I reckon young Joe Hayes, his cousin, will get it, and mebbe the old *señora's* cuss with it. What with his Escondida holdin's, looks like Joe is packin' a double cuss!"

Hatfield nodded soberly. "But there's some things, and some men, as is worse than 'cusses.' "

CHAPTER 20
BREED O' MEN

Hatfield repaired to the sheriff's office early the following morning to find out about the inquest. He found a lanky, taciturn individual seated at the sheriff's desk.

"Name's King, Neal King," the sitter introduced himself. "Uh-huh, I'm a deputy — chief deputy, I reckon, now that Fatty Wagner's due to be appointed sheriff. What's on *yore* mind?"

Hatfield told him. King dropped his booted feet to the floor and stood up, hitching his gun belt a trifle higher. He was about as thick as an average scantling and something over six feet tall. He had a cool gray eye, an angular jaw and a tight mouth that nevertheless was grin-quirked at the corners.

"Reckon the jury'll be ready to set in about half a hour," he informed Hatfield. "C'mon, we'll mosey over together."

The inquest was brief and informal, the

verdict of the jury laconic and to the point:

"These two citizens met death at the hands of party or parties unknown."

Added was a "rider" typical of a cow country jury:

"But the red hellions had ought to be run down pronto."

Up to the moment, things had been moving so swiftly that Hatfield had had little time to consider Wilfred Crane. He had instituted a few judicious inquiries, with barren results. Sheriff Dobson had known nobody answering to Crane's description; but by this Hatfield was not surprised. Crane would have undoubtedly perfected a disguise that would be hard to penetrate, knowing as he did that his part in the Guadalupe country murders was known and that he could expect pursuit.

Hatfield did not for a moment consider that Wilfred Crane was the instigator of the Big Bend trouble. He did not credit Crane with either the energy, ability or that type of mind. Crane's mental processes were subtle, cunning and cruel. He had ability, but not the kind of ability that makes for the leader of men. Crane would doubtless ally himself with a man or men more fitted to lead, to whom his peculiar talents would be of value.

"But considering that tongue cutting and

the shootings in the back and such that have been going on hereabouts, I'd say Crane is on the job and had mebbe corraled a couple more Karanks to lend a hand. Sure looks like his kind of work. Well, he'll tip his hand sooner or later, if he's mixed up in this."

Hatfield found plenty to do in the days that followed. A flume had to be constructed to convey the water from the distant fall to the scene of mining operations, and this required his personal supervision.

"It's a sight cheaper than piping, and mighty nigh as good," he explained to old Mike. "A covered flume of timbers leading to a dam above the falls will give us the head we need, and if we can get it done by the time the machinery arrives, we'll soon be set for operations.

"And, by the way, that feller Ted Harper is a mighty good man when he has somebody to show him what to do. Look the way he's taking hold. He's got a knack of getting work outa men, too, and that goes a long way to making a good foreman. Reckon it was just as well you didn't fire him."

"Notion you're right," grunted Uncle Mike. "Ted's okay, only he's got too much temper. Now if he was jest like me, he — hey! what the blankety-blank-blank-blank! Where's that blankety-blank-blank

swamper! I told him not to set that blankety-
blank gaboon way over in the corner 'stead
of where I keeps it! I've squirted tobacco
juice all over the floor! Why, that —"

Hatfield left the office grinning, with
Uncle Mike's profanity boiling out the door
in his wake. He mounted Goldy and rode
up the slope to the distant canyon and the
scene of operations.

It was a stiff climb, but Goldy negotiated
the slope with little trouble. Hatfield found
the new dam progressing satisfactorily. Harper already had his coffers down and was
pumping water preparatory to laying his
anchors of cut stone. From farther up the
canyon came the sound of ringing steel
where axemen were felling trees for timber.

"A good stand up there about a quarter of
a mile," Harper told the Lone Wolf. "We're
lucky to find it growin' so clost to the crick,
and there's a nice gentle grade, too. Easy to
snake the logs to the water's edge and float
'em down. I'm follerin' instructions clost as
to the dam."

Hatfield nodded. "I figger I've got it about
right," he remarked, explaining: "A large-
sized 'hydraulic giant,' under a head of five
hundred feet, will spout fifty cubic feet of
water per second at a velocity of a hundred
and eight feet per second. That will be suf-

ficient to disintegrate the gravel and carry it to the sluices."

"As we work up the slope we'll lose head," Harper remarked.

Hatfield nodded with pleasure at the foreman's quick grasp of the problem.

"I'm counting on that," he replied, "and later we'll build a secondary dam a mile or so up canyon. Right now we don't need it. Won't need it for some time, and it's important to get paying gravel running into the sluices as soon as possible. And," he added, "that's why I'm taking so much time to explain everything in detail to you as we go along. If I don't happen to be here when the time comes, I want you to be able to handle the job."

Harper gave him a grateful look. "I'm shore a heap obliged," he declared with feeling. "I'm learnin' more on this job than I ever learned all the rest of my wuthless life. Reckon mebbe I'll be able to hold down a good job when you're finished with me, 'stead of workin' as a drift boss all my life."

"You take hold fast," Hatfield quietly complimented him. "And," he added, fixing Harper with his level green eyes, "if you can jest learn to take hold of yoreself, to think before you act, and not go on the prod until going on the prod means something worth while, I got a hunch you'll do."

Harper reminiscently rubbed his big jaw, and grinned. "Reckon you started learnin' me that the fust time we got together!" he chuckled.

He gazed after the Texas Ranger as Hatfield rode up the canyon, admiration and affection in his eyes.

"They shore were makin' *men* the day they put that big jigger together," he remarked softly to himself.

Coma was abuzz with speculation over the new project, and visitors to the scene of operations were plenty. Among them were young Joe Hayes and Henry Lyons, who rode into the canyon together as Hatfield was returning from inspecting the felling of timber farther up.

Hayes was plainly displeased with the whole affair and suspicious, and he took no pains to conceal his attitude. Lyons was interested, and asked courteous questions. In answer to one, Hatfield gestured toward the ominous fang of rock that towered from the slope crest so far above.

"So far as I can make out, the gravel bed runs right up to the base of that pinnacle," he said. "We'll cut up the slope just as far as we can get a head to cut, which will be a long way toward the crest. Then, if the upper levels of gravel keep showing gold in paying quantities, we'll install hydraulic rams and build a reservoir up top the crest to get additional head."

Henry Lyons stared upward toward the gaunt outline of the Devil's Finger, while Joe Hayes glowered at Hatfield, muttering under his breath.

"You'll spend the money as fast as it comes outa the mine," Hayes growled at length.

Hatfield turned his level gaze upon him for an instant, then gestured to the busy scene in the canyon, and toward where far across and down the slope, other men, ant-like in the distance, were diligently preparing place for the hydraulic machinery soon to arrive.

"Mebbe," he said quietly, "mebbe I will, but it's giving good honest work to lots of men, and it's bringing good men into this district, men who are used to working for their living and who take pride in doing something wuth while. They'll make this out of the way section a lot better for their being in it, and that'll be good for Texas, and for all of our country."

For a moment Hatfield seemed to have forgotten his companions and his strangely colored eyes were bright with dreams — not dreams of self or self-advancement, but dreams of faith and pride in his fellow men and the land of his birth.

Henry Lyons stared at him, his face suddenly strained. But before Hatfield glanced back, his features had resumed their dark immobility. Young Joe Hayes fumbled with his hat, cuffed it over one truculent eye, and seemed at a loss for words.

CHAPTER 21
RIDERS OF THE NIGHT

Autumn was at hand, and the time of the fall roundups in Mescalero Valley. The air was sharp and had in it the zest of old wine. Mystic purple haze swathed the summits of the hills in tremulous veilings and the hills themselves wore royal robes of scarlet and of gold.

More than ever were the Phantoms unreal, fantastic, and the gaunt spire of the Devil's Finger seemed to pierce the hazy sky. For the first time, Hatfield saw the fiery reflected ray shoot across the valley as the sun sank in blood behind the far distant wall of the Cienagos.

"It'll keep that up all the rest of the month," said Uncle Mike Shaw. "Toward the last of the month it'll start crawlin' down the slope like a thin river of blood. That's how I discovered Escondida, by follerin' that beam of light down the slope till I come to where the rocks and earth 'peared to be all heaped up under the brush."

"Funny nobody else ever stumbled onto it during all the years, pertickler with the town of Coma only a coupla miles down there," Hatfield commented.

Uncle Mike shrugged his scrawny shoulders. "Nothin' over wonderful about it," he declared. "Look at them coma trees all up the slope — jest a wild tangle of brush and big thorns, growin' so clost together a man can hardly force his way through. No ledges up there anywhere in sight — jest the big wall of smooth rock what's the Devil's Finger.

"No ledges what look like they might have gold or silver in 'em. This shore don't look like a placer minin' section, either. It ain't. You hafta cut down deep into the gravel to turn up gold."

"Didn't washed-down gold ever show in the valley?" Hatfield asked.

"Uh-huh, it did," Uncle Mike admitted, "but you'll rec'lect the crick from the canyon where we're buildin' our dam runs down that way, and so do the other two cricks to the nawth. Prospectors allus figgered watergold what showed come down them cricks. They prospected them cricks time after time, and found a little gold, not enough wuth botherin' with. So the word got round that the cricks hereabouts warn't wuth pannin'. The funny thing to me is how the old dons caught onto this gravel belt."

"Don't figger that's over hard to come to," Hatfield told him. "That coma growth up there doesn't look so very old — fifty, sixty years at most. Chances are in their day there was very little of it on this slope. Birds eating the berries in other places start such patches as this. Without much growth, the gravel would wash out during bad rains and show the gold."

"That's right," agreed Uncle Mike. "Jest like hawgs root up the soil and when the rain washes the mounds of dirt they nose up, gold shows. Lots of placer miners have hit it rich 'cause of hawgs. Mebbe the dons had hawgs with 'em."

Hatfield chuckled but did not dispute the point.

His face grew somber, however, as his eyes fixed again on the tall bent shaft with its rounded summit bathed in bloody light. The thing had a fascination hard to explain. Hatfield felt as if it were exerting a definite pull upon his being, as if it were summoning him, drawing his spirit to its ominous dark breast.

Years of solitude, of lonely nights in the saddle with only the far high stars and the wide reaches of plain and mountain and desert for company, had whetted the Lone Wolf's perceptions, had worn thin the veil that falls between man and the deep-seated primal impulses. He had learned to obey impulses, senseless though they might seem at times. He usually called them hunches, and chuckled derisively at them, and — followed them! He followed one now.

"Uncle Mike," he asked, "ever been up to the foot of the cliff?"

"Huh? The Devil's Finger up there? Why'd anybody wanta go up there? I had hell enough scramblin' up this damn ridge through the thorns when I was huntin' for the Escondida, and cussin' myself for a fool at every step. I shore didn't have no hankering to claw my way up to that hunk o' rock with a cuss on it. I never heard tell of anybody what did, and there's lotsa *loco* gents in this section, too. Why?"

"I was wondering if it is possible to get up there 'thout fighting the slope through the brush?"

Uncle Mike grew thoughtful. "I got a notion you could cut 'crost from the Chisos Trail, travel round that bulge over to the nawth of the Finger and claw along the base of the cliffs," he admitted. "Why?"

"Oh, I've got a notion I'd like to ride up

there sometime," Hatfield replied.

Uncle Mike made some pungent remarks anent the damphoolishness of humanity in general and cowpunchers in particular, and the subject dropped.

Hatfield did ride "up there," the following day, although he made no mention of his immediate intentions to Uncle Mike Shaw. He left the Chisos Trail several miles above town and made his painful way along the base of the ragged cliffs that flanked the Finger.

The thorny brush was sparse near the foot of the cliffs, but there was enough of it to put Goldy in a thoroughly bad temper. Nor was his temper improved when, upon rounding the bulge Uncle Mike had mentioned the day before, he was forced to wade along the bed of a small stream which washed the base of the cliffs for some distance before diagonaling in a northerly direction toward Mescalero Valley.

Several hundred yards of slipping and floundering over water-smoothed stones and the stream turned almost at right angles to where it gushed from a narrow gorge, the south wall of which was the towering bulk of the Finger.

It was a weird and impressive formation, reminding Hatfield somewhat — though less in size and height — of famed *El Capitan* in the Yosemite. High, high into the blue heavens soared the great curved spire of dark granite.

From where he gazed up its shining surface it seemed to him that the gigantic mass was leaning over him, menacing him with its monstrous might, threatening to crush to powder any presumptuous being who should come seeking to fathom its grim secrets.

Slowly Hatfield rode along its slightly rounded base, the ground rising abruptly to a ridge about the middle of the spire. Far down the slope he could see the flash and glitter of Coma's windows struck by the rays of the low-lying sun. The buildings of the town seemed cut out of cardboard and propped up between the vast swell of the lion paws that curved about Mescalero Valley.

The base of the Finger was washed in shadow, but high above the sunlight struck fair upon the polished surface and suddenly the great reflected ray shot like a sword of bloody flame through the haze of the autumn sky.

Hatfield rode on, scanning the spire, the little bare, swelling plateau which skirted its base, the rolling brush-clad slope below, searching for he knew not what. Somehow, he felt, this sinister tower of dark granite played a part in this evil that was being done here in the once peaceful valley.

Suddenly he pulled Goldy to a halt and sat staring at the softer ground he was now traversing.

"Well," he told the cayuse, "old Mike may have been sincere when he said nobody ever came up here, but he shore was a heap mistook!"

The spongy soil in the shadow of the spire was deeply scored by hoof prints, many of them, and of varying age. Hatfield instantly noted that while some were the clean-cut scars of irons, the majority appeared to have been made by unshod horses. Slowly he rode on, studying the tracks.

"A lot of somebodies have been traveling past here," he mused, "and going and coming. Looks, too, like they been in a habit of stopping here on this level space."

He glanced downward again, toward where Coma was misty with distance, and growing unreal in the fading light.

"Wonder if they could be seen from down there anywhere?" he asked himself.

He decided quickly that, due to the inward slope of the little plateau and the height of the growth which fringed its lip, they could not. He was just about the middle of the curving wall of the spire, now, and he turned his glance toward its gleaming surface. His eyes traveled over it and his interest quickened. He sent Goldy close to the gently curving face and sat staring.

Undoubtedly at this point the surface had been scraped by the hand of man. Hatfield could plainly see the marks of rock-cutting tools. A section of the stone had been chiseled away, leaving a smooth, flat expanse. And, scored deep in the living rock, were characters in precise lines.

"Spanish," muttered Hatfield, leaning close, "Spanish words cut in the rock, and not so very long ago, either."

Peering in the dim light, he translated the brief message:

The stream of the North and the stream of the South shall join ere murdered blood cease to cry out for vengeance.

For long minutes Hatfield stared at the cryptic message, his dark brows drawing together until the concentration furrow was deep between them. He shook his black head, shoved back the brim of his wide hat and rumpled his crisp hair in perplexity. The words didn't seem to make any sense at all. But the painstaking care with which they had been cut so deeply into the stone, involving no mean amount of labor, scouted the idea that they were nothing other than the work of an idle moment.

"They mean something," Hatfield growled, "and something mighty important, or I'm a heap mistook." He repeated under his breath, "Stream of the Nawth, stream of the South, now what —"

Abruptly he turned Goldy's head and rode straight to the lip of the plateau. He was opposite the exact center of the Finger, at the apex of the gentle curve, and at the crest of the ridge, and could glance along the plateau in either direction.

Gazing to the south, his eye caught the gleam of hurrying water. In another instant he had traced it to its source. A big spring boiling up from under the south wall of the Finger, and hurrying southward to dive into the black mouth of a canyon. He turned and glanced north. There, too, was the gleam of swift water — the little stream through which he had waded his horse a short time before, the stream that ran in a northerly direction before swinging around toward Mescalero Valley.

And between the sources of the respective brooks swelled the mighty bulk of the

Devil's Finger, with a steeply rising grade from either source.

"Over there's the 'stream of the Nawth,' and over this way is 'the stream of the South,' " he muttered, "and the way they're headed now, it shore will be an almighty long time before they get together!"

He turned and stared at the grim inscription, shaking his head dubiously. Jim Hatfield understood the irresistible Latin impulse to be dramatic. But he understood, too, the deathless memory, the grim tenacity of purpose of the land of *mañana* where blood feuds are concerned. It did not seem strange to him that some dark-faced son of the fiery South should cut this sinister promise and threat into the ageless stone, seeing in the weird pinnacle bathed in bloody light, a symbol fitting to his mood. Nor did he in the least discount the evil that might grow therefrom.

" 'Pears like somebody hereabouts has a score to settle," he mused.

He wondered if he had by chance hit onto the explanation of the apparently senseless killings and torturings that had plagued the valley of late, and which had brought him, Hatfield, to the scene. The idea appeared preposterous. So far as he had been able to learn, Ralston, Sheriff Dobson and old

Mike Shaw had no enemies worth mentioning.

Dobson in his official capacity might have incurred hatred. But Hatfield considered the reason for the sheriff's murder as fairly obvious — to recover the odd-calibred gun that might have served to identify the killer or killers of Bruce Ralston, owner of the Bowtie ranch. The other outrages Hatfield had learned of appeared to be wanton depredations without rhyme or reason.

Hatfield rode again to the edge of the plateau and sat gazing toward Coma and the mouth of the Mescalero Valley. The sun had set, the fiery reflected ray had vanished, and the lovely blue dust of the dusk was beginning to sift down from the hills. Obeying a sudden impulse, he wheeled Goldy and rode southward toward the dark mouth of the canyon into which the stream vanished.

It was a fairly wide canyon whose sloping sides tumbled sharply through a welter of growth toward its distant floor. The stream dived over its steep box with a silvery roar. The box end was much lower than the side walls, the northern one of which was the dizzy loom of the Devil's Finger.

Along the base of the Finger a trail ran, and Hatfield could see that it had been

213

recently traveled. As far as he could see in the dying light, the rock wall extended, with the growth-covered slope climbing steeply to join it and with the trail flowing along its base.

"An old-timer, this track," he muttered, "and 'less I'm a heap mistook, it runs almost due south and crosses the Mexican line. Notion it was one of the smuggling routes in the old days — may be yet, for that matter. Shore has been traveled of late. I reckon the brush growing up thick on the slope above Coma changed a lot of things hereabouts. Chances are this trail was used a lot of years ago, 'fore the revolution swept all the section south of the Big Bend clean of folks and spreads.

"Then, with nobody to come this way from the south, it wasn't used any more, the brush grew up and hid where it crossed over to join the Chisos and folks up here forgot all about it. Rather common happening all along the border, and pertickler in this out of the way section. Which is one of the things that makes smuggling and rustling and robbery so darned easy, and Texas Ranger work so darned hard! And I bet a peso the gents what have been riding this goat track of late haven't been doing it for any good."

It wasn't really a goat track; that Hatfield quickly realized as he rode along it in the shadow of the towering wall. It was level and wide, actually a road in dimension. Soon he decided it really *was* a road, or at one time had been. The marks of tools were plain on the rock wall to his left, and the surface was smooth and free from boulders, although in places grown with grass and clumps of brush.

The height of the brush, a slow-growing species of chaparral, aroused Hatfield's interest.

"Been there a long, long time," he mused. "Funny the folks who took such pains to build this track woulda let brush stand in the middle of it."

Suddenly he gave a low whistle. He had hit on the obvious solution to the mystery.

"The road the old dons built!" he exclaimed. "The road they used to carry the gold from Escondida down into Mexico. They didn't use the Chisos Trail — wasn't any Chisos in those days. That came later, with the cattle that was run into Mescalero Valley, years and years after old Castro was killed by the Indians and the mine mouth covered up.

"Chances are this road hasn't been used since then. Or until the gents who made

215

these tracks I'm riding over right now happened along. What I'd like to know is why they're using it now. Well, it's getting pretty dark. Reckon I'd better call it a day and head back to town."

Hatfield rode on a little farther, however, toward where the trail swung around a bulge in the rock wall, beyond which he could not see. He reached the bulge, followed its gradual curve. And suddenly Goldy pricked his ears in an attitude of listening.

Hatfield heard it, too, a muffled click and pad. His hand tightened on the bridle. And at that instant horses swung around the bulge only a few yards distant.

For an instant there was stunned inaction on both sides. Then Hatfield saw the quick gleam of a drawn gun. He was slewing sideways in the saddle when flame gushed toward him.

Hatfield's mind worked at racing speed. To wheel Goldy and ride back the way he had come would be tantamount to committing suicide. The road ran straight as an arrow for hundreds of yards and the light was still good enough for accurate shooting.

He would be drilled dead center before he had covered a double score of feet. To shoot it out with a dozen or more gunmen would be but to make a glorious and utterly senseless end. Before the crash of the report followed the whine of the passing slug, the Lone Wolf acted.

"On, Goldy!" he thundered, clamping the sorrel's barrel with legs like bands of steel. Straight into the flame of the roaring guns raced the golden horse.

What Hatfield did was the last thing the horsemen expected him to do. With yells of pain and terror they scattered before his roaring guns. Horses clanged over the edge of the trail into the growth; others slammed against the cliff; their riders howled and cursed.

Into their demoralized ranks crashed the raging golden horse, teeth bared and clashing, ears laid back, eyes rolling, red nostrils flaring. Hatfield slashed right and left with the barrels of his smoking guns. He had a wild, blurred vision of distorted dark faces, rearing broncs, flashing guns and frantic pack mules bearing unwieldy burdens.

A skyrocketing dazzle of intense white light, a numbing shock, and he knew he was hit. But even as he reeled in the saddle he was clear of the mad welter of men and horses. Down the trail crashed Goldy. Reeling, swaying, blood streaming down his face, Hatfield twisted in the saddle and flung his last bullets at the milling mass.

With a roar like a thousand thunderclaps the very mountains seemed to reel and rock. A volcano-blaze of reddish flame hurled back the shadows. Goldy sprawled in his stride, all but swept from his feet by a hurricane blast of air that seemed to scorch his coat. He screamed with fright.

Through the appalling tumult knifed a soaring shriek of agony. There was a crackling and rumbling, and a series of sodden thuds. The darkness swooped down on a screeching babble of voices and the whinnies of terrified beasts.

With his last failing strength, Hatfield tugged sharply on Goldy's right rein. The sorrel swerved, staggered, caught his footing by a miracle of agility and went floundering and crashing down through the heavy brush that covered the steep slope.

Shots were fired from above, and the bullets whined close; but an instant more and the tall brush hid him from view as he slithered onward toward the distant canyon floor. Hatfield mechanically holstered his empty guns and swayed forward, clutching at the horn with nerveless fingers. His face buried in the coarse black mane, he lay along the sorrel's neck, his thighs still clamping him in the saddle.

As the slope leveled off and Goldy came to a sobbing halt in a little cleared space, the Lone Wolf swayed gently, relaxed, slid from the sorrel's back and lay silent and motionless, his bloody face buried in the grass.

Chapter 22
"Miracles"

For many hours Jim Hatfield lay unconscious beside his patient horse. It was Goldy's uneasy nuzzling at his face with velvet lips that finally brought him around. He opened his eyes, closed them again quickly as pain stabbed like a white-hot knife. For minutes he lay fighting a deadly nausea; then, as he breathed deeply of the cool night air, his aching head began to clear. He opened his eyes once more and stared up at a blazing net of stars. Beside him the sorrel loomed dark and gigantic.

"All in one piece, old-timer?" Hatfield inquired shakily.

Goldy gave an explosive snort that undoubtedly bespoke thankfulness and relief. Then he whinnied softly and pawed the ground with a dainty hoof.

Hatfield sat up, with an effort, still fighting against the roiling sickness. He was stiff and sore and his teeth chattered with cold.

He could feel a crusting of dried blood on his face and as he raised a shaking hand to his head, he winced at the contact of his fingers with torn, ragged flesh.

Resisting the pain, he explored the cut with a fingertip.

"Just creased — shallow furrow — and it's stopped bleeding," he muttered thankfully.

To his ears came a sound which he recognized as the ripple of water over stones and he was conscious of a raging thirst. He got to his feet and stood swaying. Then, leading the horse, he staggered off in the direction of the sound.

A moment later he reached the bank of the little stream that ran through the canyon. Side by side, he and the horse drank deeply of the clear, cold water. Hatfield bathed his blood-crusted face and tied a water-soaked handkerchief about his injured head.

The chin strap had held his hat in place despite his fall, and he found that, by tilting it a little more than normally, the bandage would be hidden from view. He removed Goldy's saddle and bridle and allowed the cayuse to roll and then crop the grass.

Hatfield meanwhile rolled a cigarette and sat at the edge of the stream and smoked, his strength coming back and the ache in his head abating. Finally he stood up, shook himself and put the rig back on Goldy. Carefully reloading his guns, he mounted and sent the sorrel at the slope.

"Let's go up and see what pulled the mountain down," he said.

It was a hard and painful pull up the brush-clad slope, but Goldy made it as the silent dawn spread its red mantle over the lonesome mountains. In the strengthening light, Hatfield stared at the deep crater hollowed out in the center of the trail.

The cliff wall was splashed with ominous dark splotches that had not been there the night before. In the bushes nearby he found the shattered body of a man, a man whose lank black hair and swarthy face interested him greatly.

He found a second body not far from the first one, with a black hole in the middle of the forehead. This second man was of ruddy complexion and had bristly red hair. A third body crumpled against the cliff was of dark coloring similar to the first. There was a similarity in the clothing of all three — fringed buckskins and moccasins. Hatfield also noted a crumpled sombrero heavy with silver ornaments.

"Belonged to the red-headed jigger," he

deduced. "Reckon t'other two went bareheaded, Yaqui style."

He found two dead horses and his green eyes narrowed as they rested on the ragged wounds where the brands had been ripped away. There was also a dead mule, its head torn from its shoulders, and scattered about were fragments of flesh, including a portion of a mule's leg, upon the hoof a worn shoe.

Hatfield speculated these grisly remains. "Reckon that pore devil of a mule was packing the load of dynamite my bullet set off," he mused. "Now what in blazes, do you s'pose, an owlhoot outfit such as that shore musta been was doing packing a load of dynamite in an *aparejo?* Were they figgering on blowing a bank vault or a strongbox in a stage coach? I wonder!"

Further search disclosed the shredded remains of an *aparejo* or pack sack. Its contents had evidently been carried away, but partially hidden by a clump of brush, and doubtless overlooked in the darkness, was a steel drill and the head of a pick. Hatfield examined both with frowning brows.

"Tools for rock work, or I'm a heap mistook," he declared. "That drill's the proper diameter for driving a hole to receive dynamite cartridges. Now what *does* this mean?"

Hatfield went over the ground with meticulous care, but found nothing more of interest. Very thoughtfully he mounted the sorrel and rode on up the canyon, eyes and ears alert, hands close to his guns.

But there appeared no trace of the dark riders, although the damp ground in shadow of the Devil's Finger showed signs aplenty of their passage. What puzzled Hatfield greatly, however, was the lack of evidence of their entering the Chisos Trail.

"Smart," he decided at last, "too damn smart! Took no chances and covered their tracks so's nobody could tell just where they hit the trail or which direction they traveled. Wonder where in blazes they are now."

A thought struck him and he turned Goldy and again splashed through the stream and climbed the slope of the narrow plateau. With minute care he examined the soft ground. Finally he straightened up and nodded with satisfaction, but with a perplexed furrow wrinkling his brow.

"They came back this way last night while I was snoozin' under that bush down there in the canyon," he declared to Goldy. "I was outa my senses for quite a spell, all right, but not long enough for that outfit to go very far and get back again, certainly not down Mescalero Valley any distance or to

Welch. Coma musta been where they were heading for.

"But why pack dynamite and tools to Coma from down Mexico way? That's like carrying hay on the prairie in summertime. Plenty of dynamite in Coma, tools, too; but," he added reflectively, "maybe they didn't wanta buy them there. Which shore proves for fair they were up to no good with that load of blasting powder. Wonder if they had more'n one load?"

Hatfield wondered, too, if the mysterious riders had conducted a search for him on the return trip, but decided that doubtless they had not. They would, it was reasonable to believe, have assumed that he had made his escape, was holed up in the brush, or that his dead body was lying somewhere in the wilderness of growth.

In either case it would have been folly to comb the canyon in the darkness. He was devoutly thankful that Goldy was a silent horse and not given to advertising his presence by neighing when his fellow-kind were in the neighborhood.

Upon reaching Coma, Hatfield decided that his wound did not require medical attention. So, after dressing it himself, he went to bed. Darkness was falling once more when he awoke to the sound of shouts and cracking guns. For a moment he lay listening, then he called a question to Ted Harper, whom he could hear thumping about in his adjoining room.

"Trail herd and roundup crews comin' into town," Harper called back through the thin partition. "It's pay day on all the big spreads hereabouts and at the mines, too. Batches been arrivin' all day, and loaded for bear. Feller, it'll be hell in this pueblo tonight!"

As Hatfield ate his breakfast in a nearby restaurant, he was inclined to believe that Harper had not overstated. Mounted cowboys whooped and clattered up and down the street. The sidewalks were crowded, the air tingling to a whirl and babble of sound. Every saloon, and there were plenty of them, blazed light and blared what was intended for music. Raucous voices bawled something claimed to be song, and others just as raucous bawled curses at the singers. Men bellowed with mirth and bellowed with wrath.

The rumble of deep tones blended raggedly with the high-pitched voices of women and their shrill laughter. There was a constant clinking of bottle necks against glass rims. On the dance floors heavy boots clumped and high heels clicked. The clatter and rattle of roulette wheels slid smoothly over the snaky slither of cards and the sprightly chuckle of dice galloping across green cloth. There was a whine of fiddles, a soft thrum of guitars, a pert tumping of banjoes.

Gold clinked musically at the gambling tables and rang sharply on the bars. Swaggering punchers and bearded miners sat across from waxen-faced gamblers in long black coats and snowy shirt fronts. There was a flash and glow of silks and satins and the gleam of white flesh where the dance hall girls whirled in the arms of brawny partners who cavorted with all the grace and abandon of frolicking bears.

This was Coma's big night of the year — the roundups finished, the trail herds loaded and rumbling east and north, money burning holes in pockets and itching to be spent. The hundreds of mine workers were there, too, with a month's pay to blow in one riotous night of pleasure.

Gold black with blood and salty with the sweat of utter toil was to be thrown away in wild abandon. What the devil! Plenty more where this came from! Do you want to live forever? What for? I'm a younker tonight — tomorrow I'll be an old man! Belly up, boys, this one is on me! Down the hatch! And another one for a chaser!

Hatfield finished his meal, smoked a leisurely cigarette and sauntered out into the street. His green eyes were lazy, indifferent, traveling over the jostling throng with apparent aimlessness, just as his tall form passed with the same apparent aimlessness along the creaking board sidewalk. But the long green eyes missed nothing, and they were searching — searching for dark faces they had caught but distorted glimpses of the night before.

But a glimpse of a face was enough for the Lone Wolf. The features would be indelibly engraved on the tablets of his memory, and instantly recognized no matter what the place, company or conditions in which they were next encountered.

Slowly he made his way up the crowded street, easy, assured, walking with the lithe grace of youth and strength and perfect coordination. Men, and women, turned to gaze at him, attracted by the rhythmic perfection of his motion, impressed by the lean, bronzed face that was too full of man-power to be handsome in the strict sense of the word, but wonderfully attractive in its magnetism and vitality.

Bleak-faced individuals with hard and watchful eyes glanced at him in sideways fashion, taking in at a single swift sweep the slim, powerful hands, the filled double cartridge belts snugged about the lean, sinewy waist and the heavy guns hanging low against the muscular thighs, the black butts flaring slightly from his hips and always seeming very near to those quiet, deadly hands.

"Salty," was the general verdict, "plumb salty, and a cold proposition!"

And these watchful wanderers of the wastelands, these men with their backs to the past and not caring to look to tomorrow, wondered covertly who the tall two-gun man might be, but they carefully took no steps to find out.

Shortly before midnight, Hatfield encountered Neal King, the taciturn deputy sheriff, who greeted him with a nod of, for him, unwonted cordiality.

"Gonna be some night 'fore she's over," remarked King. "Listen to her howl, will you; and you ain't heard nothin' yet! The boys are too busy gettin' drunk as yet to really act up. Wait'll the red-eye gets to boilin' in their bellies, and then hunt a hole and pull it in after you!"

Hatfield chuckled. "Does look sorta up and comin'," he admitted. "Where's Wagner, the new sheriff?"

King grunted. "Him and Joe Hayes is pallin' round together somewhere," he replied. "Chances are they're over to Ruby's by now. Usually are by this time of evenin'. Escolita does her fust dance at midnight."

"What's Ruby's, and who is Escolita?" Hatfield asked as he fell in step with the deputy.

"Ruby's is Ruby's saloon and dance hall run by Ruby, who musta been one helluva swell looker oncet upon a time and ain't so bad now," replied King. "Escolita is about a hundred pounds of white fire and black lightnin' and essence of volcano wrapped in the skin of the damnedest purtiest gal that ever came outa *mañana* land.

"She's what makes old fellers like me wish we was young again and young fellers like you give up tryin'. I even believe she could make Fat Wagner stop eatin' and get thin. If Joe Hayes warn't plumb *loco* 'fore he saw her the fust time, he shore is now."

"Say, where is this here Ruby's?" demanded Hatfield. "I'll judge all this for myself."

"Come along," invited King, "I'm amblin' over that way now. Dust off yore eyes, feller, you're gonna see miracles!"

Ruby's proved to be the biggest and brightest saloon Hatfield had yet visited in

Coma. It sat near the western end of the main street, which was a section of the Chisos Trail that wound through the heart of the cow town. Beyond was the wide reaches of Mescalero Valley shadowy and mysterious in the starlight. Behind the saloon ran a dark alley.

The bar ran the full width of the sprawling room and was glittering with mirrors and many bottles of various hues. Four busy bartenders sloshed drinks into waiting glasses and wiped their perspiring faces on their white aprons.

To one side were poker tables, roulette wheels, a dice table and a faro bank, the latter largely patronized by swarthy Mexicans in black velvet trimmed with silver. Their wide sombreros boasted gay bands and much silver ornament. The majority, Hatfield deduced, were from the big haciendas in the southwest, though doubtless some came from the Mexican-owned ranches near the mouth of Mescalero Valley.

The greater part of the floor space was given over to dancing. Here all was a whirl and glitter of changeful color. Girls in scarlet gowns, in white satin, in blue, danced with miners whose brawny shoulders were encased in woolen shirts of various gaudy hues. Lithe young cowboys wore neckerchiefs of yellow or wine or purple. Mexican dandies provided a rich, dark touch with their somber velvet. Here and there gleamed the immaculate shirt front of a gambler who had deserted the tables for the moment to relax in the company of the lady of his choice.

It was a laughing, chattering, good-tempered crowd, for the moment at least. The temper might well change as the night wore on and the fumes of drink steeped the brains of the dancers. Now all was gayety.

Hatfield sensed a subtle undercurrent of anticipation, especially on the part of the younger men. Glances were cast in the direction of a curtained doorway near the far end of the bar. An open space led from the doorway with its drapes of smoldering red velvet to the center of the dance floor.

Hatfield turned at the sound of Neal King's voice at his elbow.

"Hatfield," the deputy was saying, "I wanta make you acquainted with Ruby. Ruby owns these here diggin's."

From his great height, Hatfield gazed down upon the woman King had escorted through the crowd. He smiled gravely, removed his hat and bowed, the light of the hanging lamps seeming to strike a blue shadow on his thick hair, so black it was.

"It's shore a pleasure, Miss Ruby," he acknowledged in his deep, soft voice, and took the white hand she proffered in his sinewy fingers.

The woman glanced at him strangely, and hesitated perceptibly before replying.

"Ruby's sorta sizin' you up," King chuckled.

The woman smiled with a flash of white teeth.

"Yo' all are suhtanly sizable enough," she said in throaty, drawling tones. "Can't say as I ever saw a taller man 'cept ol' Majah Dickson down home in Noo O'leans."

"You are from Louisiana, Miss Ruby?" Hatfield asked courteously.

Ruby shrugged her white shoulders.

"I'm from most any place," she replied, a sudden hard note in her voice.

Hatfield glanced down at her curiously. She was a striking woman, superbly tall. She could not have been more than thirty years old, he judged, but in her large blue eyes with dark circles under them was something that hinted of untold age. Her face must have been lovely once, and it held the haunting ghost of beauty still, with features of clear-cut classic regularity. Her hair was dead gold, with highlights of burnished copper.

Hers, Hatfield instantly sensed, was an irresistible power possessing a base and mysterious affinity for men, a power linked with evil wisdom and utter ruthlessness. And yet, in the depths of the fine eyes was something not altogether corrupt and degraded, the shadow, perhaps, of a spirit stifled and starved but still crying weakly and persistently for expression.

Acknowledging this, he smiled down at her, and Ruby instinctively smiled back. Then she turned away, signaled with a white, beringed hand to the orchestra leader. The music stopped, attendants began clearing the floor of dancers.

Ruby raised her hand again; the orchestra swayed into a lilting melody, the red velvet curtains fell back, and Jim Hatfield saw the *"miracle!"*

CHAPTER 23
HANDS IN THE DARK

Through the space between the drawn curtains flashed a girl in a flame-colored gown. And for a fleeting instant, Hatfield almost felt it was a living flame wafted on the invisible wings of the music.

She was slender and dainty, with curves where curves were in order, and vibrant with the vitality of silvery water leaping in the sunshine, and graceful with the grace of a flower swaying in the dawn wind, and cool and sweet with the coolness and sweetness of moonlight glancing on the first green leaves of spring, and warm with the pure warmth of starlit summer nights, and mysterious with the mystery of autumn's brooding hush.

She had long, dark eyes and there seemed to be red shadows in their depths. Youth and beauty and magnetism and charm — she had them all. And as a glorious crown, a womanly sweetness and sympathy that even the least observant could not fail to sense.

Hatfield turned to Neal King as a roar of applause shook the room.

"You win," he chuckled in a low voice, "my eyes need dustin'!"

The girl danced, and she danced with Latin abandon and the utter sureness of self that bespeaks the artist. Hatfield instinctively realized that there was nothing of exhibitionism in her performance. It was the spontaneous, elemental dancing of a child, a pure impulse of youth and spirit and pulsing life.

She flung back her curly head and laughed with a laugh like a peal of little silver bells, her teeth flashing white and even, her red lips, which were devoid of paint as were her creamily tanned cheeks, parted, her dark eyes crinkling at the corners.

Hatfield glanced down at Ruby, who was standing a little apart. Her cold, regular features had softened and there was a tenderness in her blue eyes, and pride. Neal King interpreted his glance.

"Ruby watches over that gal like a eagle over a 'dopted chick," he said in low tones. "Escolita dances *for* the trade, but not *with* anybody. Where's she from? Down Mexico somewhere. Shore she's Mexicon, or rather,

I'd say, old Spanish blood. Shore a funny thing that she should be dancin' here in a Coma honkytonk. Say, look at Joe Hayes, will you!"

There was a table near the edge of the dance floor, a table covered with bottles and glasses. Escolita soared to its top like a wind-whirled leaf. Amid bottles and glasses she danced, and her tiny flashing feet disturbed not one.

Standing beside that table was young Joe Hayes, gazing up at her. His handsome, obstinate face had softened, the sullen lines were smoothed out, and his very soul showed in his hungry eyes. He seemed utterly fascinated, and his gaze was fixed on the girl's face as to a magnet.

Escolita paused in her dance, her warm young breast heaving, her eyes laughing at the applause. She glanced down at Hayes, met his longing look, and for a moment Hatfield sensed a peculiar light in her dark eyes, a subtle change in the expression of her sweet mouth. Then abruptly she flung her head back, drew her little figure up scornfully and blighted him with a flashing glance.

Hatfield heard snickers in the direction of the table, saw Joe Hayes flush darkly. For an instant his lips trembled. Then he dropped his eyes, his shoulders drooped and he turned and slouched away into the crowd. Somebody laughed, the music blared forth afresh, and Escolita went on with her dance.

Again she paused for breath, laughing, sweeping her merry glance over the heads of the crowd.

Hatfield saw her stiffen, saw the red of her lips fade to the gray tinge of fear. Her eyes widened — great pools of dark light, fixed staring.

Hatfield, taller than any man near him and able to see over their heads, followed the girl's shrinking stare.

In the door stood Henry Lyons, his dark face inscrutable as always. His gaze was fixed on the little dancer in an impersonal way, in it something, perhaps, of curiosity. Indifferently he turned away and began speaking to the man at his side.

Hatfield's gaze, swinging back to Escolita, saw the color bloom high in her cheeks once more, saw her laugh in a wild, reckless way, leap from the table top and dance merrily back to her dressing room behind the velvet curtains.

The whole episode had taken but a fleeting moment of time, and Hatfield doubted if anyone other than himself had observed it.

"What scared her?" he mused. "Was it Lyons, or that husky, broken-nosed gent he was talking to? Lyons didn't seem to pay her no mind a-tall, but I'd swear she was looking straight at him. Well, one thing's shore for certain, the Hayes feller is plumb roped and hawgtied!"

Leaning against the bar, sipping his drink, Hatfield watched the colorful scene. Occasionally he addressed a remark to the taciturn King, who answered with grunts or a terse comment. Both being silent men, they got along very well together.

Hatfield was feeling a growing respect for the lean, saturnine deputy and discovering in him an unsuspected fund of dry humor and a shrewd insight into men and their motives, as revealed by his infrequent but pithy observations.

King suddenly jerked his thumb down the bar. "See Joe Hayes and some of his gang are shore takin' on a skinful," he said.

Hatfield glanced in that direction and placed the young ranch owner in the middle of a group of about his own age. His companions were reckless appearing young men with roving eyes and an assured air. All were drinking plenty, and Hayes, it appeared, more than anyone else.

Young Joe's face was flushed, his eye baleful. He downed a glass of raw whiskey as if it were water, and hammered on the bar for a refill.

Hatfield studied his companions, and abruptly his green eyes lost their warmth and seemed to subtly change color. He turned to King and remarked in casual tones:

"Those fellers all ride for Hayes?"

"Most of 'em," grunted King. "Couple of 'em don't, I figger, that is 'less he hired 'em recent for round-up work. That little dark hombre I ain't seen before. The tall jigger with the scar I've seen pallin' round with Joe oncet or twicet. Name's Durade. I think he works for a spread over to the mouth of the valley. I seem to rec'lect that Henry Lyons fired him a while back over somethin' or other — too much drinkin', I reckon. Lyons is a serious sorta gent and sorta upright. Don't stand for much foolishment."

Hatfield continued to study the countenance of the tall man. His full beard and his hair, worn so long that it rested on the collar of his coat, were golden in hue. What could be seen of his features was deeply tanned by sun and wind. On the left side of his face was a great scar and his left eyelid lay flat over an empty socket. The bridge of his nose was broken and driven inward. His figure was lanky, loose-jointed but sinewy. His gestures were assured, he said little and appeared to be holding his liquor better than his companions.

Hatfield speculated the scar. " 'Pears to have been made by a bullet," he mused, "the same one that knocked his eye out, and busted his nose, the chances are. A mighty hard scar to cover up, too, mighty hard, but that missing eye —"

King's hand on his arm distracted him and he turned to his companion.

King was speaking again. "Young Joe picks out a prime lotta hellions to 'sociate with," said the deputy. "If he keeps on the way he's been goin' for the past year, he's gonna end up in somethin' bad or I'm a heap mistook. He owns a nice little spread, and has quite a interest in old Mike Shaw's mine, pertickler now that Bruce Ralston has left him his holdin's.

"Then there's the Bowtie, which Joe is takin' over. That's the best spread in the valley. Ralston gettin' cashed in by the Injuns was a sorta break for Joe, all right. 'Side from Uncle Mike and mebbe ol' Train Beverly, I reckon Joe'll be about the best fixed gent in Mescalero Valley. That is, if he don't drink or gamble it all away. Pity somebody can't get holt of him and straighten him out 'fore he goes plumb bad.

"I've a notion that little gal Escolita could do it, but she shore treats Joe like dirt under her feet. The way he looks at her, I've thought once or twice he'd jest necherly carry her off some night whether she wanted to go or not. He shore is sweet on her."

"How long has Escolita been dancing here?" Hatfield asked.

" 'Bout a coupla months," King replied. "She come in here on the stage from Welch one day. Fust feller she met was Clate Dobson — spotted him for sheriff by his badge, I reckon. She steps right up to Clate and says in that soft voice of hers, 'What is the worst place in thees town where girls dance?' Well, Clate was so plumb flabbergasted he spoke right out 'thout thinkin'. 'Wal, ma'am,' says Clate, 'I reckon Ruby's up to the head of the street figgers to be.' *'Gracias,'* says the li'l lady, and toddles right up to Ruby's, and Ruby hires her, and shore takes her under her wing."

Hatfield chuckled, but his eyes were somber, and the concentration furrow was deep between his black brows.

An argument was in progress down the

242

bar. Joe Hayes appeared to be urging the scar-faced man to something, and the scar-faced man kept shaking his head. Finally, however, his objections appeared to be overcome. He nodded, albeit reluctantly, and after another drink, the group noisily left the room.

A little later King announced his intention of returning to the office.

"Call may come in," he explained, "and it's hard to tell where Wagner is liable to be — celebratin' his appointment in some eatin' house, the chances are."

Hatfield lingered at the bar a little longer and then also took his departure. He wandered from one saloon to another, drinking now and then, stopping once or twice to give a roulette wheel a few whirls. He was still seeking faces, and not finding them. Once he remarked cryptically to himself:

"Wonder if there could be two gents in this district with a half-moon sliced down the cheek?"

The night was well advanced when Hatfield wandered back to the neighborhood of Ruby's. At the mouth of a dimly lighted alley which intersected the cross street just below the saloon he paused. Somewhere up the dark passage he heard the sound of an opening and closing door, and a quick tapping of light feet. Then his pulses leaped to the sound of a swift scuffle and a muffled scream.

It was a woman's voice!

Chapter 24
Coyote Pack

Hatfield leaped into the alley and ran swiftly up it, hugging the walls of the buildings, where the shadow was deep. Directly ahead was a confused blotch of twisting solider shadows. The Lone Wolf ran silently as the gray wraith for which he had been named, but in the darkness he could not see the empty bottle someone had dropped in passing. His foot hit it and there was a sharp jangle of breaking glass.

"Look out!" somebody called hoarsely. Then the woman's voice, instantly muffled:

"Help!"

Hatfield rushed the group. Flame gushed from the darkness and he felt the wind of the passing slug. He dared not fire back for fear of hitting the woman. A dark form loomed within arm's reach and he lashed out with all his strength. The impact of his fist on flesh and bone jarred his arm to the shoulder. There was a choking groan and the sound of a falling body.

He weaved sideways, struck at another shadow. A hand clutched his shoulder, a knife gleamed in a chance ray of light and he felt its burn along his arm. With a back-handed blow he knocked the wielder sprawling. He hurled a third man from him with a vicious twist of his wide shoulders and as the group whirled about he saw the slight form of a girl struggling with a man who held her. Hatfield lunged for him, his fingers closed on a throat and he put forth every atom of his great strength. With a choking gasp the man let go the girl and clawed at his wrist with both hands.

Hatfield reeled under a stunning blow from behind, struck out blindly with his free hand and felt his fist go home. He staggered back against the wall, red flashes storming before his eyes.

A little hand thrust into his, gripping his finger, pulling, urging.

"Come!" shrilled a sweet voice. "Queeckly! They will recover — they will keel you — there may be others!"

Still half dazed by the blow on the back of his head, Hatfield stumbled obediently after his guide, who tugged and hauled, directing his dragging feet into a narrow opening between the two buildings. His shoulders brushed the walls on either side. He was hauled about, tugged into a second narrow passage that ran at right angles to the first. A moment more and he stumbled against a step.

"Up three!" panted his companion. "Now the two more. And the three. Wait!"

Numbly obedient, fighting hard to retain his senses, Hatfield heard a key rattle in a lock. A door opened and he was urged forward. He heard the door close behind him and waited in black darkness.

A light flared and revealed a neat, clean little room, plainly but comfortably furnished. Hatfield shook his head to clear it and stared about. Standing before him, heaving from her exertions, her dark eyes still wide with fear, but with a smile beginning to twitch at the corners of her red mouth, was the little dancer of Ruby's — Escolita!

"Oh," she exclaimed breathlessly, "you are the tall *señor* who watch Escolita dance on the table!"

Hatfield grinned. "Reckon there were quite a few gents watching you, so far as I can rec'lect," he replied.

"But I do not see them," the girl said. "I look over the heads, always, but your head I cannot look over."

Hatfield laughed outright at this naive remark. Then he abruptly sobered.

"Any chance of that outfit down there following you here?" he asked.

The girl's smile faded, but she shook her dark head. "I do not think so," she replied. "Thees my room — where I live — and I came by the back way from the dance hall. Always I slip out and hurry here when my work is over. Nobody sees me."

" 'Pears somebody saw you tonight," Hatfield told her dryly.

Escolita again shook her head. "No," she declared. "They do not see. They were waiting in the alley for someone and see me when I come out the back door."

"Any notion who that somebody mighta been?" Hatfield asked her softly.

The little dancer lowered her eyes. "I — I know not, for sure," she faltered.

"Ma'am," Hatfield said quietly, "it appears to me that somebody sorta wants you — wants you bad enough to grab you in the dark. You any notion who *that* is?"

The girl glanced up wildly. "No, no, I tell you I know not!" she declared passionately.

But Hatfield knew she lied. He shrugged his broad shoulders.

"Okay, li'l lady," he told her. "If you won't, you won't. But I got a mite of good advice for you — don't slip out the back way any more. Go out the front door and stay in the light. Better still, allus have somebody you can trust go with you. I might not happen along, and be lucky, next time."

"Lucky!" The girl caught hold of the latter phrase of his statement. "Lucky! *Señor,* you were — you say it how — superb. You were wonderful, and I — I thank you."

Hatfield regarded her gravely. "You can thank me best by following the advice I gave you," he replied. "You're too nice a girl to have anything happen to."

Escolita smiled and dimpled. "You really think so?" she asked demurely, with downcast eyes.

"Uh-huh," Hatfield assured her, "and so do others, I figger. For instance, that good looking young feller who stood by the table while you danced."

The girl started as if struck, and Hatfield saw her red lips quiver. Then she drew herself up haughtily.

"Of heem I prefer not to speak!" she said with icy emphasis.

"Huh?" wondered Hatfield. "Why you so on the prod against Joe Hayes?"

"Do not discuss heem!" she burst out passionately. "He is of — of the — the — he is one — I must not!"

She was sobbing now, crumpled down on a couch, her piquant little face buried in her slim, lovely hands. Hatfield leaned over and patted her soothingly on the shoulder.

"Come on, now, forget it," he urged. "You've had a bad experience and you're all upset. Wash yore face and go to bed like a good girl. I'm leaving now — don't calc'late you'll need any more help."

Escolita came off the couch in a lithe spring. "Oh, I am horrid," she exclaimed contritely. "I have not really thanked you for what you did and — oh! There is blood on your hand!"

"Just a knife scratch in the arm," Hatfield deprecated, trying to conceal the reddened member behind his back.

But Escolita showed she possessed a will of her own. Before he knew for sure what was happening, Hatfield found his sleeve rolled up and his sinewy left arm bared. The cut was really little more than a graining of the skin by a sharp knife point, but Escolita insisted on bandaging it and applying a soothing ointment.

"You will come see me dance again?" she asked as Hatfield headed for the door.

"I 'spect," he told her. "Chances are I'll drop into Ruby's soon. By the way," he added, his hand on the knob, "do you know a feller named Henry Lyons?"

The color drained from Escolita's expressive face. "I have heard the name," she replied slowly. "Why — why do you ask?"

"Oh, I just saw him standing in the door looking at you tonight," Hatfield answered carelessly. "Good night, ma'am."

"Now what in blazes is this all about?" he mused as he followed a corridor that led to front steps and a street that paralleled the one onto which Ruby's saloon fronted. "Who were those hellions that tried to grab her in the alley? Bunch of jiggers out for a lark? Doesn't seem likely. What was that Neal King said about Joe Hayes looking at the girl as if he'd like to carry her off?

"Shore wish I'd got a good look at those hellions I tangled with, but I wasn't seeing over well after I got that thump on the head." He felt tenderly of a sizable lump that swelled under his hair.

"One thing's certain," he told Goldy as he made sure the sorrel was cared for properly, "she's sorta interested in young Joe, and plumb on the prod against him for some reason she isn't telling; and, she's scairt stiff of Henry Lyons. Plumb nice district this. Indian drums, night riders packing dynamite, murders, torturings, and a dancing

251

girl what knows plenty and won't talk."

Then he added with apparently utter irrelevance, "Wonder how that scar-faced jigger, Durade, would look with a nigh black complexion and black hair 'stead of red?"

As Hatfield wearily sought his bed, he suddenly glanced up at the starry sky. Was that low mutter thunder from an unseen cloud? No, it was not thunder. From somewhere in the direction of the black spire that was the Devil's Finger pulsed an angry roll and rumble of drums!

CHAPTER 25
RANGER CRAFT

Dust and sun! Purple haze shrouding the hilltops. A huge brassy ball high in the murky heavens blazed down on the white ribbon of the Chisos Trail, glancing from leaves that were already aflame with color. Amid the wanton riot of autumn's scarlets and golds, the pinon pines and other evergreens were somberly dark, almost black. Crag and chimney and pinnacle were mellowed and softened by the haze.

But the white surface of the trail was hard and uncompromising, ashimmer with heat waves, amid which the dust devils whirled and danced. In great clouds the dust rolled up from beneath the grinding wheels of four huge freight wagons which lurched and rumbled up the trail.

To each wagon were attached eight straining mules, and on the high seat perched a sweating, swearing teamster who whirled his eighteen-foot lash about his head, sent the multiple thongs hissing and crackling over the backs of the mules and threatened them with destruction dire and dreadful.

The wagons were heavily loaded, heaped high with ponderous packing cases. Upon the rough boards of the cases was stenciled in large black letters:

AUSTIN HYDRAULIC
MINING MACHINERY CO.

The brassy sun reached the zenith, began to drop down the long slant of the western sky shining obliquely through the haze. The light assumed a reddish hue which stained the dust clouds as would a blown mist of blood. The teamsters wiped their sweating faces with bared forearms, cursed the dust, the sun, the mules, earth, eternity, life itself.

They were alert, watchful men, those teamsters. Their eyes roved over the trail ahead, scanned the distant wall of stone across the deep gorge whose nether lip the trail hugged. Much of their attention was directed toward the steep, brush-covered slope which swelled upward from the dusty trail.

Now and then they cast glances into the dark depths of the gorge, the brush-covered floor of which was hundreds of feet from the overhanging lip of the trail. They were armed with gun and knife and had the air of men who knew how to use both.

Up and up wound the trail, with the awful drop of hundreds of feet of nothing at all on one side and the swelling, brush-covered slope on the other. The mules were nervous, jumpy, with pricking ears and switching tails. They seemed to sense events in the making.

The nervousness communicated to the drivers. They glanced over their shoulders, studied the slopes ahead, their watchfulness redoubled. But just the same they were utterly unprepared for what happened.

Without the slightest warning, the dark, silent slope ahead woke to tumultuous life. A wavery line of pale flame flickered along the straggle of brush. There was a staccato crackling, then the shrill whine of passing lead.

A mule of the leading team went down, kicking and squealing. Another sprawled over its body. Instantly where there had been efficient order was pandemonium. The mules bucked and squealed, rearing back, plunging in their harness. The huge wagon slewed around, its rear end crashing against the slope.

The driver, yelling with terror, dropped

the reins and leaped from the high seat. Madly he fled down the dusty trail as a second ragged volley crashed from the brush. His companions tumbled from their perches and pounded in his wake. They rounded a bend, dived into the growth and went scrambling up the slope.

Soon they were hidden by the tall brush, snugged beneath bushes, peering with wide eyes at the happenings on the trail below. One, a big Irishman with flaming red hair and a truculent blue eye, pulled his gun from its sheath. A companion snatched it from his hand.

"Lay low, you fool!" he hissed. "One shot and you'll bring the whole band onto us. We can't fight twenty armed Injuns! Look at 'em come skulkin' outa the brush. There's more'n twenty, and they're still comin'!"

Another teamster spoke in a hoarse whisper. "Them hellions is full-blood Yaquis! Look the way their hair is cut hangin' over their eyes. If they come lookin' for us we're good as scalped and chopped up right now."

"They won't come," replied the man who snatched the Irishman's gun, "they'll know we're holed up in the brush somewhere if we ain't hightailin' it down the trail. It wouldn't pay 'em to try and root out four jiggers with guns. They're after the loads, that's all. Look at the scuts shovin' them cases over the edge into that damned canyon!"

The dark-faced, buckskin-clad raiders had swarmed from cover and into the trail. While some, with ready rifles, scanned the slope and the downtrail with watchful eyes, the others hauled the big cases from the wagons, straining and grunting with effort, and hurled them into the dark depths of the gorge. The crash of their striking the rocks hundreds of feet below sent echoes pounding along the opposite wall.

"This is a dommed crazy business makin' this trip, anyhow," grumbled the big Irishman. "We'll be lucky to git outa it with our hair."

His companion jingled coins in his pocket. "We got paid good for it, didn't we, and in advance?" he demanded. "Me, I'm gonna have me a high ol' time in Coma tonight. Wuth takin' a little chanct for."

"There goes the last case," grunted the Irishman, "and there go the spalpeens up the trail. Look, there's others leadin' horses outa the brush. Begorry, they didn't take the mules or shoot 'em!"

"Of course they didn't," grunted another. "They don't need mules, and even a Injun is leary of murderin' hoss critters for nothin'. There they go, ridin' away. We've seen the last of 'em. What you fellers gonna do? Me, I'm ketchin' me a mule and ridin' to Coma."

"Begorry, and I'll go with yez," declared the Irishman. "I started for there and I don't perpose to let any dommed Injun keep me from afther goin' to where I started."

The other two teamsters decided to ride back to Welch, taking the empty wagons, tandemed together, with them. The two dead mules were freed of harness and shoved into the canyon.

Dusk was falling when the two teamsters flogged their weary mounts into Coma and reported what had happened. Uncle Mike Shaw cursed them and everything else.

"Where's Hatfield?" he demanded. "Harper, find Hatfield and bring him here."

An hour later, however, Ted Harper, the foreman, returned alone.

"Scoured the hull damn town," he reported. "Can't find hide or hair of him. 'Pears he was last seen ridin' outa town last night with that deputy sheriff, Neal King."

Uncle Mike swore some more. Harper departed to attend to his multiple duties. A few minutes later Joe Hayes stormed in.

"What'd I tell you!" he shouted, his face black with anger. "Didn't I say this was all damphoolishness! Didn't I tell you that slick jigger Hatfield was a maverick? All that 'spensive machinery gone to glory! Thousands of dollars wasted! For what?"

It was typical of peppery old Mike Shaw that when he faced an angry man, he himself grew cooler. He fixed Hayes with his filmy blue eye and spoke quietly, but with finality.

"I'm still runnin' Escondida," was all he said.

Hayes' face twisted into a sneer. "Yeah? I reckon you are, for a while, anyhow. Yeah, I know you own a controllin' interest, but listen, I'm gonna own enough of this shebang to rate a say as to how the money's spent. I done had a talk with Lawyer Hutchinson and he told me I'll be able to get a minority stockholder's court order for an accountin' as to what's done with the money comin' outa Escondida. I'll own enough to be entitled to a say."

Uncle Mike stared at him. "You done gone *loco?*" he demanded. "What the devil you talkin' about?"

"What'm I talkin' about?" purred Hayes. "Jest this: Clate Dobson owned a hefty holdin' in these diggin's, didn't he? Well, Clate left a will. That will was drawed in favor of Bruce Ralston and his heirs. Lawyer Hutchinson says they ain't no doubt about it I'll get what Dobson left. Then we'll see!"

Hayes stalked out, leaving Uncle Mike staring at the wall. For a long time the old man sat silent in his chair. Then he spoke, as to someone across the table.

" 'Pears Bruce and pore ol' Clate gettin' cashed in turned out mighty profitable to Joe Hayes."

The two teamsters with the empty wagons rumbled into Welch shortly after sunset. With many gestures and much profanity they told their story. Then they unhitched their exhausted mules and sought food and rest. And as the dark closed down, a second caravan of big wagons rolled out of Welch and climbed the Chisos Trail.

This time there were eight of them, all heaped high with ponderous packing cases, upon the side of which there was no stenciling. Before and beside and behind them rode armed men, alert, watchful.

Heading them was Neal King, the taciturn deputy sheriff. Beside him rode Jim Hatfield.

It was Hatfield who first reached the Escondida building early the following morning. He was some distance in advance of the rumbling wagon train. Early as it was, Uncle Mike Shaw was already at his desk. His old face was lined and weary, but he bounced up bristling as Hatfield entered the office.

"Where the blankety-blank *you* been?" he demanded. "Did you hear what happened? All our hydraulic machinery is at the bottom of Talkin' Water Canyon!"

Hatfield stemmed his tirade with a gesture. "Nope," he said soberly, "nope, that isn't machinery at the bottom of Talking Water Canyon. That's just some boxes of rocks and scrap iron. I figgered those hellions might try something like that, and I sorta put one over on 'em. You see, I couldn't very well ask for a sheriff's posse to guard that shipment from Welch to here just because I had a hunch.

"Wagner wouldn't have given me one, and King couldn't very well go over his boss's head 'thout something definite to act on. King sorta conveniently happened to be in Welch when those teamsters brought their empty wagons back and nacherly he felt sorta justified in swearin' in a posse right off and heading back with us to Coma."

"But the machinery?" demanded Uncle Mike. "Where the blankety-blank is the machinery?"

Hatfield gestured through the open window, toward where the wagon train was turning off the trail and approaching the emplacements that had been prepared for the hydraulic giants.

"There's yore machinery," he said quietly. "All safe and ready to set up. It'll be operating in less'n a week."

CHAPTER 26
RED LIGHTS
AND ALTAR CANDLES

Several busy days followed for Jim Hatfield, during the course of which he supervised the unloading and erecting of the hydraulic machinery. He did find time to ascertain that the canyon through which ran the ancient road really did provide a short cut to the Mexican border.

But the canyon opened out before it reached the line. The road was lost in the shifting sands of a strip of desert and there was no way of telling where the marauders might have crossed the river, or even if they had continued to the border, or turned toward some other objective before reaching it.

Once or twice he saw the scar-faced man, Durade, in the company of young Joe Hayes, and he felt sure that the pair were covertly observing him and discussing him. Of the faces he sought he saw nothing. Nearly two weeks had passed since his visit to Ruby's when he again entered the garish saloon, about midnight. As he passed through the swinging doors, Escolita swirled onto the floor to do her specialty dance.

Escolita was the same in her youth and loveliness. But this time her dance was different. It was more wanton, wilder, rife with a subtle lure. Hatfield noted that the girl's face was unwontedly flushed. He noted, too, that now instead of keeping her gaze fixed above the heads of her audience she met glances boldly, her black eyes narrowing, the red shadows in their depths flaring to the surface.

Hatfield sensed a studied effort to inflame, to excite the emotions of the men who crowded about the dance floor and clapped and cheered.

The dance ended, but Escolita did not swirl back through the red velvet curtains. Hatfield saw her mingle with the other dancers on the floor, a drunken cowboy's arm about her trim waist. He caught snatches of remarks from the men at the bar, heard derisive laughter. He saw young Joe Hayes, his face haggard, his eyes burning, staring after the dancing girl.

Hayes took a step in her direction, but the scar-faced Durade gripped his shoulder with cruel fingers, swung him about, spat words into his ear. Hayes growled and muttered, but permitted Durade to shove him through the swinging doors. The darkness swallowed the pair.

Hatfield gazed after them, a speculative light in his green eyes, the concentration furrow deepening between his brows. His glance shifted back to Escolita, and the speculative light intensified. He turned at a touch.

Ruby was standing beside him. She looked older than on his previous visit and in her fine eyes was a new look of uncertainty. Hatfield felt the hand on his arm shake. She, too, was staring at the dancing girl.

"I — I don't know what's come over her," she said, a break in her throaty voice. "She's — she's changed. She's took to drinking — she never did that before. Tonight, when I tried to talk to her in her dressing room, she — she slapped me, flung me off, refused to listen."

Ruby turned to the Texas Ranger, and now there was stark misery in her eyes.

"Hatfield," she said, her voice almost a whisper, "Hatfield, it's hell to love something, and watch that something go to the devil! To see that something, good and sweet and pure, become what — what *I* am! My God, I believe I'm going crazy! I — I believe

I'm going to — to commit murder!"

Hatfield looked down at the woman with the haunting ghost of dead beauty still on her face. He sensed what she once was, understood her love for the girl who was still what *she* once had been. His level gaze held her, dominated her.

"Wait," he said quietly. "Things aren't always what they look to be. Wait."

Ruby bent a long searching glance upon his face. She drew a deep, quivering breath.

"Yes," she said, "I'll wait."

Hatfield finished his drink and left the room.

The turbulent hours passed in Ruby's saloon. Escolita finished her last dance, changed to her simple street costume. But she did not slip out the back door. She walked through the crowd to the street, head held high, glancing to right and left, her lips smiling, her slim hips swaying. As she passed through the swinging doors, more than one man moved as if to follow her. But she moved so swiftly that she had whisked around the corner in an instant.

Reaching the side street she ran, swift and lithe as a deer. She turned another corner and a moment later tripped lightly up the steps that led to her room. She turned into the corridor, at the far end of which a light

266

burned dimly. She approached her door, and the tall figure of a man stepped from the shadows and confronted her.

Escolita gasped, shrank back, one hand pressed tightly against her red lips.

The man was Jim Hatfield.

CHAPTER 27
THE TIGHTENING LOOP

For a trembling moment the little dancer stared at Hatfield. He held her eyes with his level gaze, motionless, not speaking. Finally he gestured to the key she held in the hand pressed to her mouth.

"S'pose we go inside," he said quietly.

Escolita hesitated, but his eyes dominated, compelled her. Obediently she unlocked the door, entered the room. Hatfield entered behind her, waited until she had lighted the lamp, then closed the door and stood with his back against it. His eyes had never left her. They were steady, grave, but not unkind. The girl trembled, stared back at him, fascinated.

"Well, *señorita,*" he said in his deep, drawling voice. "What's the idea of sending yourself to hell just to get even with somebody?"

The girl shrank back from him as if he had struck her. She stared, her eyes widening with something akin to terror.

"W-what do you mean?" she gasped.

"I mean," Hatfield said, "that you are deliberately setting out to be revenged on somebody, no matter what happens to yourself in the process. What's the idea, and who is it?"

The girl shrank back still farther. She dropped on the couch, covered her face with her hands. Her shoulders shook with a wild, uncontrolled sobbing. Suddenly she looked up, her eyes wild, burning.

"You are right!" she cried. "I *will* be revenged. I'll drag his proud name in the dust. Wait! Wait until I tell everybody in thees terrible town who I am — my name. I, who bear his name, dancing in the vilest place in thees vile town, laughed at, leered at. Already I am talked about. Already men are beginning to wonder. Even she — Ruby — my *amigo* — is not sure. Men talk of Escolita. Soon they will talk of another name.

"What do I care what happens to me? I hate him! I will have my revenge. He deserted my mother, broke her heart. She died of a broken heart. He has sunk low — lower than even I thought possible. He is friend to those he should hate. But he had pride — pride in his old and honored name. Through that pride I shall strike. I will have my revenge!"

Jim Hatfield understood the Latin mind, the Latin temperament. He understood the scorching pride of fiery Spanish blood, the boundless capacity for hate, the undying desire for vengeance for wrong done. He knew that under the wild, incoherent words of the girl was a terrible fixed purpose. She meant what she said. Only Spanish blood and Spanish heritage could conceive this subtle scheme of vengeance. Only Spanish tradition and way of thinking could fully understand and appreciate its strength.

"Uh-huh, and send yoreself to hell getting it," he replied to her frantic declaration.

She stared up at him defiantly.

"And send others there at the same time!" he continued.

"Others?"

"Yes," Hatfield pursued remorselessly. "Young Joe Hayes for one. He's making a fast trip. And Ruby — Ruby's already there, but you mighta pulled her back."

The girl's lips were white, her eyes great pools of horror.

"No — no!" she whispered.

Hatfield leaned forward, held her with his eyes. "Tell me," he said softly. "Tell me his name, his real name."

For a moment her glance met his, then

her eyes dropped and she stared dully at the floor. Slowly she shook her head from side to side. Hatfield gazed at her for a moment, recognized the futility of argument, and left the room.

Outside in the street he paused and stared up at the stars paling in the first flush of dawn.

"I gotta work fast!" he muttered. "There's still loose ends banging about, and they've gotta be tied up fast. That hellion is smart, almighty smart. He'd slip through a loose loop like a greased yearling. I gotta tighten my rope, and I haven't got much time."

Hatfield went back to Ruby's for a nightcap before turning in. The dance floor was deserted, the crowd at the bar thinning out. He found a poker game in progress at a table near the end of the bar.

The players were Sheriff Walt Wagner, Henry Lyons, the scar-faced Durade, Joe Hayes and a couple of lean men in cowboy dress whose faces were unfamiliar. The stakes were evidently high and the intent players vouchsafed Hatfield hardly a glance. He leaned against the bar, toying with his drink, and watched the game.

Joe Hayes was losing, Hatfield sensed. The young ranch owner's face was flushed, his eyes red from drink and lack of sleep. He peered at his cards in a scowling way and made frequent nervous gestures. The set of his coat seemed to annoy him and he shoved the left lapel back with a petulant sweep of his hand.

As the coat fell back for a moment, Hatfield caught a dull gleam of metal. His eyes narrowed slightly and he regarded Hayes thoughtfully. Joe wore a heavy belt gun slung low on his left hip, the butt turned to the front, the mark of a cross-draw man. But, Hatfield now knew, he also rode a shoulder holster.

Hayes continued his fidgeting. His moving and jostling appeared to irritate the quiet Lyons. He said something sharply to the young man and struck the table with his hand. The sound seemed hard, metallic, yet his hand was empty.

Hatfield's eyes narrowed still more. "And that jigger's got a gun up his sleeve, derringer, probably," he muttered. "And *he's* wearing a belt gun, too. What an outfit! Heeled and double-heeled, and watching each other like hawks."

Lyons' coat was brushed back, revealing the big gun in its scabbard. A section of the heavy cartridge belt was also revealed. Hatfield scanned the gun idly, frowning a little at the smooth ivory handle of the six: the

Lone Wolf was prejudiced against pearl and ivory handles.

"Too slick," was his verdict, "liable to turn in the hand; and they catch the light at night, too, and give the other jigger something to shoot at."

His gaze shifted along the gleaming rims of the cartridges in the belt loops. Suddenly something peculiar about those belt loops attracted his attention. He stared at them intently. Then he abruptly finished his drink, placed the empty glass on the bar and sauntered across to the little sandwich counter, passing so close to Lyons' chair as to almost brush against him.

Hatfield did not pause, but his keen glance focused on the belt loops, missing no slightest detail of their construction. He ordered a sandwich at the counter, raised it to his mouth with a steady hand. But in the shadow of his wide hat, his long, black-lashed eyes seemed acrawl with green fires.

CHAPTER 28
"ABOUT ALL"

The installation of the hydraulic machinery was completed. The huge brass nozzles on their ball joints which permitted horizontal and vertical play stood like gleaming cannon, their muzzles directed at the towering gravel bank of the mountain side. On each platform stood men whom Hatfield had carefully instructed in the operation of the metal monsters. Other workmen clustered nearby, tense, interested, waiting for the Lone Wolf to give the word. The dam in the canyon was finished, as was the long covered flume of massing timbers.

It appeared that all of Coma and Mescalero Valley were present for the beginning of operations. In the forefront stood, among others, young Joe Hayes, his face flushed, his eyes bloodshot. Beside him, lean, lounging, passive with the deadly passiveness of an unsheathed rapier, was the tall man with the scarred face — Durade, Hayes' constant companion.

Henry Lyons, dark, impassive, stood a little apart with Sheriff Walt Wagner. It seemed to Hatfield that in Lyons' dark, inscrutable eyes was an expression of sardonic amusement. Hatfield wondered, a trifle uneasily, why. He hesitated to give the word to begin operations, experiencing a nameless feeling of disquietude.

Everything, he felt sure, was as it should be; everything was in perfect working order; nothing had been overlooked. He cast a last searching glance over the equipment, and as he did so, he permitted himself a covert chuckle.

"Jest what the devil am I, an engineer or a Texas Ranger?" he asked himself with amusement. "I figgered to come over to this section as a ranger, but things appear to have gotten sorta scrambled."

His face set in grim lines. "I took the right track, though," he congratulated himself. "Just another thread or two, and the loose ends are tied up. I'm mighty nigh ready to risk the final play, mighty nigh ready!"

With a shrug of his broad shoulders he abruptly faced about, grasped a lever with his powerful hand. The men at the nozzles stiffened alertly, gripped their controls. Hatfield threw the master lever which turned the mighty head of water into the lead lines. The men at the nozzles moved.

With a hissing roar, eight-inch streams of water shot from the giants, striking the gravel bank with a shattering crash. Clouds of dust arose, instantly breaten down beneath showers of rainbowed spray. Torrents of muddy water cascaded down the slope, choked with gravel and earth, swirling their burden toward the waiting sluice boxes. The assembled crowd gave a rousing cheer.

For several minutes Hatfield let the huge jets of water roar and storm. Then he signaled to the nozzlemen, who closed their throttles. The roar subsided, stilled. The ensuing silence was almost painful.

"Reckon she works, eh, gents?" shouted old Mike Shaw, his wrinkled face beaming with excitement.

The tall Durade said something to young Joe Hayes. The pair turned their gaze full upon Hatfield. Hayes' face twisted into a sneer. He laughed jeeringly, an offensive, personal note in his sardonic mirth.

Jim Hatfield's eyes suddenly blazed green fire. Two long strides and he had reached Hayes. His sinewy hand shot out, gripped the ranch owner by the throat. Clean off his feet he lifted the heavy man, and shook him as a wolf shakes a rat. He spoke, his voice cold as steel grinding on ice.

"Hayes, I've stood all from you I'm gonna stand. You're nothing but a spoiled brat, a good-for-nothing whiskey guzzler. A wuthless bawl-beller profiting from the work of better men. If I hear anything more outa you, I'm gonna tie you in a double bowknot and ram you down yore own throat!"

With a final shake that rattled the man's teeth like castanets, he flung Hayes from him. Young Joe sprawled on his face in the muddy gravel, plowed up several yards of it, rolled over and lay gasping, a sight to gaze upon.

"Look out!" howled Uncle Mike Shaw.

But Hatfield had seen, from the corner of his eye. He leaped sideways with pantherish grace, ducked under the whizzing knife Durade had drawn, and knocked Durade a half-dozen yards straight through the air.

Durade lay where he fell, his bloody face buried in the mud. Hatfield swept the frozen crowd with a bleak glare that was like a glacial wind. For a tense instant he stood lance-straight, towering, commanding, thumbs hooked over double cartridge belts, slim, deadly hands scant inches from the flaring butts of the big black guns. Then he relaxed, dropped his hands, spoke in his normally soft and drawling voice:

"Well, I reckon that'll be about all."

There was silence.

Young Joe Hayes got painfully to his feet, wiped the blood and mud from his face, stared at the tall Texas Ranger. Suddenly his face broke into a grin that was almost boyish. He looked Hatfield squarely in the eye. He spoke, and his voice was hearty, respectful, devoid of malice.

"Uh-huh, big feller, you said it: I reckon that's about all!"

Squaring his shoulders, and without a glance at the unconscious Durade, he turned and strode sturdily down the slope toward Coma. Jim Hatfield gazed after him, and his bleak, strangely colored eyes were suddenly all kindness.

Chapter 29
Disaster

Several busy days followed. Fiercely the hurtling streams of water tore into the towering slope, bringing down untold tons of earth and gravel. Old Mike exultingly reported that the sluice boxes were already showing gold.

Hatfield felt that he could safely turn over to Ted Harper this job that had unexpectedly been placed upon his own broad shoulders. He was almost ready to act, but not quite. The master-thread of his close-drawn web still eluded him — that master-thread of motivation which was all-important, without which, firm in his grasp, he dared not take the final step.

"That hellion is smooth," he repeated to himself, "smooth and deadly. It'll take a plumb tight noose to hold him."

And ever, the baleful, flaming ray that reflected from the polished surface of the Devil's Finger dropped lower and lower over Mescalero Valley, until the red lance of light seemed barely to clear the treetops of the slope.

Hatfield had not been to town for two days. He had eaten and slept at the scene of operations, sharing a hastily constructed bunkhouse with men who constantly attended the machinery. Late the third night he entered Ruby's.

Ruby herself saw him the moment he passed through the swinging doors, and hurriedly joined him at the bar. Her face was strained, there were new lines visible, and the circles under her blue eyes were darker.

"Something terrible happened last night, Hatfield," she told the Texas Ranger. "This town is getting even my nerve."

"How's that?" Hatfield questioned.

Ruby looked hurriedly about, moved a little farther down the bar, to an unoccupied space, and spoke in low tones.

"Last night, just before she was going on for her last dance, Escolita discovered that the heel of one of her slippers was cracked. One of my girls, the little redhead they call Flame, offered to go to Escolita's room and get another pair. She slipped out the back way, and when she didn't return I sent a swamper over to Escolita's room to find out why. He found out!" Ruby shuddered, and her rich voice choked in her throat.

"Yes?" Hatfield prompted quietly.

Ruby continued, with apparent difficulty. "He found Flame — in the hallway — dead. She'd been stabbed!"

Hatfield regarded her for a moment, his eyes coldly gray.

"Ruby," he said at length, "you still got some influence over Escolita, haven't you?"

"Yes — some," she hesitated.

"I want you to use it," Hatfield told her, "use every bit of it to keep Escolita with you — day and night — every minute."

Ruby stared at him, her eyes dilating with horror.

"You — you mean that knife was meant for — was meant for —"

"Yes," Hatfield finished the sentence for her. "It was meant for Escolita. Can you keep her with you?"

The golden woman was suddenly transformed. The air of hesitation, of uncertainty left her. She straightened, her blue eyes burned. Once again she was the Ruby who ruled men, who with her white hand quelled trouble in the toughest joint in a tough cattle town before it got fairly under way. She hissed like a snake.

"I'll keep her!" she promised between set

teeth. "I'll keep her if I have to break that white neck of hers!"

It was late when Hatfield got back to the camp. Thoroughly weary, he went to bed and almost instantly fell asleep. He awoke with a start. The first gray light of dawn was stealing through the windows. His ears still rang to a distant roaring explosion followed by rumbles and crashes, which swiftly died to silence.

Other men were sitting up in their bunks, asking questions, making exclamations.

Outside sounded a sudden shouting, a dwindling of the hiss and roar of the giants worked by the night force.

Hatfield leaped from his bunk and began dressing with swift efficiency. Boots pounded outside, the door was flung open. An excited man pierced through the gloom, spotted Hatfield.

"Boss," he shouted, "the water's stopped comin' down the flume, and there was one helluva racket up toward the canyon a minute ago. It — listen!"

From far up the darkling slope of the mountain sounded a throb and mutter that swelled to a triumphant roll and died away.

"Drums!" exploded the man. "Injun drums! Them red devils have raised some new hell and shoved a chunk under a corner, or my name's not Casey!"

Hatfield kept Goldy near him at the camp, sheltered under a lean-to. He saddled and bridled the big sorrel at lightning speed.

"Bring the gang after me, with guns," he ordered Ted Harper, and galloped away in the direction of the canyon.

It was broad daylight when Hatfield reached the canyon. There he found a scene of wild destruction. The dam and the flume were buried beneath thousands of tons of stone which choked the canyon to a height of many feet. The cliffs on either side showed colossal shatterings. They had been rent and riven by terrific explosions of dynamite.

Hatfield's face was bleak, set like iron. He stared at the jumbled ruin, visioning as he did so that blazing explosion in the canyon through which ran the ancient road of the Mexican gold seekers of long ago.

"So that's what they were packing dynamite over this way for, and not buying it in Coma! They mined the cliffs with charges, waited until the construction was all finished and things looked fine, then set it off. Well, it shore looks like somebody doesn't want Uncle Mike Shaw to make money outa the Escondida Mine. I've got a hunch I can name the somebody, even if I can't prove it

283

yet. But in the name of blazes, why?"

All day long he searched the canyon for clues to the marauders, examined the destruction wrought, estimated the extent of the damage. Late in the day at the Escondida building, Uncle Mike Shaw received his discouraging report with dull apathy.

"Looks like things is sorta finished," he admitted. "I ain't got the money to clean up that mess and build new rams and flumes, and I doubt if I can get it outa the mine. The tunnel workin's are barely payin' expenses now. 'Sides, after this happenin', I figger I won't be able to have the full say as to what's done with the mine money.

"Joe Hayes owns a hefty holdin' now. He seems to have sorta improved some since you walloped the daylights outa him, ain't drinkin' so much and ain't pallin' around so much with that snaky Frank Durade. But he's stubborn as hell and I figger I won't be able to swing him into my line of thinkin'."

There was nothing Hatfield could say, at the moment. A silence ensued. Together they stood in front of the mine building staring up the slope toward where the Devil's Finger glowered balefully in the red light of the setting sun.

"Look," old Mike suddenly exclaimed. "Look, Hatfield, and you'll see how I come to find Escondida. It's got to the time of the year when the sun's swung round so's the last light from it slants up and hits the curved under-side of the Finger. 'Stead of shootin' a ray 'crost the valley, it beats right down onto the slope in line with the mine mouth. Watch, now."

Hatfield fixed his gaze on the baleful finger of stone. Suddenly from the curved surface a fierce red ray shot downward at a sharp angle. Squarely upon the growth-covered slope it beat. The thorny coma brush seemed to leap into living flame. Every twig and berry stood out clear and distinct, and through the straggle showed glimpses of a beetling cliff a score or more of yards in height, to which the growth clung raggedly.

"Watch, now," repeated Uncle Mike. "In a minute it'll start crawlin' down the slope toward the mine mouth."

Before Jim Hatfield's eyes suddenly blazed words from the dying message penned by old Fernando de Castro, many, many years ago:

. . . the treasure is there — where the red ray falls . . . the wealth shall lie hidden and the mine will remain indeed *La Mina Escondida!*

285

"The treasure *and* the mine!" Hatfield muttered. "He kept talking about them like they were two different things — 'where the red ray falls'!"

Uncle Mike glanced up. "Eh?" he questioned, bewildered.

Hatfield came out of his absorption with a start. He shot staccato sentences at the old man.

"Quick — pencil and paper — don't ask questions — quick! I can't take my eyes off it!"

Gurgling amazed profanity, Uncle Mike hurried to obey. Hatfield, his intent gaze never leaving the spot where the red ray focused, seized them from him. With swift, skillful fingers he began making a sketch as the ominous red light started to move down the slope.

With the eye of the trained engineer and the uncannily gifted plainsman, he measured heights and distances, estimated the angles of declination and ascent, the length of the base of the giant triangle formed by the Devil's Finger, the ray and the slope.

"Got it!" he exclaimed exultantly. "Uncle Mike, it's a hunch — nothing much more — but it's a hunch that ties up mighty nice with some loose ends. It's a hunch that says you're mighty soon gonna be sitting on top of the heap, and I'm gonna take a long ride!"

CHAPTER 30
MURDERER'S GOLD

The following day, Jim Hatfield and Uncle Mike Shaw rode up the Chisos Trail. The track was empty when they cut away from it at the head of the slope and they felt sure they were not observed. They splashed through the little stream, climbed the rise of the shallow plateau and reached the middle of the great wall of rock that was the Finger.

Uncle Mike stared at the Spanish inscription chiseled in the stone and swore weakly. But like Hatfield, he understood and appreciated the deadly threat, the sinister purpose embodied in the vainglorious wordage.

Hatfield rode to the lip of the plateau. He drew forth the sketch he had made and studied it thoughtfully.

"Directly in line with where we are and an eighth of a mile or so down the slope," he announced.

Uncle Mike scanned the steep, brush-clothed, boulder-strewn and broken slope with the eye of a prospector thoroughly familiar with such a terrain.

"Don't think the horses can make it," he decided. "I reckon it'll be shanks mare from here on for us."

Hatfield nodded agreement. Always solicitous of his horse's welfare, he dismounted and led Goldy and old Mike's cayuse through the brush until he reached where the little stream diagonaled down the slope.

After some search, he found a little clearing on the near bank, grass-grown, hemmed in by tall, thick growth. He removed the rigs from the horses and hobbled Shaw's mount. Goldy, he knew, would not stray. Here the animals were provided with water and grazing. They would be comfortable and hidden from view. As an afterthought he detached his sixty-foot lariat and took it along with him. It might come in handy during the scramble down the steep slope.

The descent proved to be irritating and painful because of the thorns and the sharp stones. But not particularly difficult until near the end of the distance Hatfield had estimated. They paused on the up of a steeply sloping wall of ledged and shattered rock. Uncle Mike shook his head dubiously.

"If we get outa this without busted necks,

we're gonna be lucky," he declared.

The edges, the irregularity of the cliff face and the stout coma trees that sprouted from every crevice made the scramble to the bench below less difficult than they anticipated. Scratched and bleeding and nursing bruises, they finally made it and paused on the flat surface of the bench to catch their breath.

Hatfield again consulted his drawing. "Right about here is where I figger the ray focused," he said. "Now let's go over this section and see if we can find signs of anything buried or hidden."

They went over the ground, every foot of it, ranging far to the right and left against the chance of error in the drawing or Hatfield's calculations, and found — nothing.

The hours passed, the sun slanted down the western sky and still they persisted. Finally they joined company at the spot where Hatfield maintained the fiery ray had focused. Uncle Mike wagged his grizzled head pessimistically.

"Looks like we're nosin' a cold trail, son," he declared. "Reckon the old don was sorta flighty when he wrote that message; reckon that 'counts for the funny way it was worded. I'm scairt that the Escondida Mine was the only treasure he was talkin' about.

"There shore ain't no sign of anything bein' buried hereabouts, or any hole in the ground where it mighta been hid. The brush might hide a mound or markin' from anybody lookin' down from above or up from down below, but when you get down close to the stems like we are, it's easy to see it don't hide nothin'."

Hatfield did not reply. His keen gaze was roving back and forth across the terrain they had so painstakingly examined, probing, analyzing, taking into consideration every blotch or seam in the cliff face, the position of every tuft of brush growing from crack or crevice. Suddenly his glance fixed on the sloping wall a score or so of yards to the right of where they had scrambled down it.

Clumps of brush dotted its surface but much of the stone was in plain view; and now that the low-lying sun was casting its rays full upon the surface, he noted something heretofore overlooked. The face of the cliff seemed at this point to step forward slightly. There was no break apparent in the irregular wall, but Hatfield was sure it was no optical illusion. He turned and scrambled swiftly toward the spot, Uncle Mike trudging along some distance behind, muttering disconsolately in his whiskers.

Hatfield reached the spot opposite the formation that had excited his interest. He scrambled up the slope until he was close to the wall of rock. Suddenly he gave an exultant shout.

"What you found, son?" demanded Uncle Mike, clawing and skittering through the brush.

"Look!" Hatfield exclaimed. "No wonder we overlooked it. A man could pass within five feet of the cliff and never notice it. See — the rock folds back on itself like a doubly creased sheet of paper."

Puffing with effort and excitement, Uncle Mike joined him and together they stood peering into a narrow crack that split the face of the cliff at so sharp an angle as to almost parallel the outer surface. That slight stepping forward of the rock wall to the right was the only visible clue to its existence, and, as Hatfield declared, it was practically unnoticeable even to a person passing along the foot of the cliff.

Together they entered the crack, followed it for a score of paces, the light swiftly growing fainter. Abruptly the narrow passage turned at practically right angles. They faced into a black cave mouth from which exuded a chill, clammy breath.

Uncle Mike Shaw hung back. "Son," he

remarked dubiously, "do you really figger there might be somethin' wuth while in that hole? Looks mighty dark and lonesome to me."

Hatfield smiled. "I'm still follering a hunch," he said, adding, "let's go back outside a minute 'fore we crawl in any farther."

A little distance from the crevice was a gully whose sides were covered with flowering weeds. There was an abundance of dry sotol stalks in evidence and Hatfield gathered an armful of convenient lengths. He knew they made excellent torches.

"Okay," he told Uncle Mike, who likewise provided himself with stalks. "We'll be able to see where we're going, anyhow. Hit the trail, pardner!"

Together they entered the black mouth of the cave. The flame of the torch Hatfield carried revealed smooth, glistening walls and a dense arch of rock a few feet above their heads. The floor of the cave sloped gently downward. The floor was littered with boulders of various sizes and was rough and uneven.

For more than an hour they followed the turns and twists of the passage. Always the slope was downward, gentle but persistent, until Hatfield knew that they were deep down in the bowels of the mountain. The air was dank, but fresh enough, and there was a steady, unnatural draft that bent the flame of the torch inward as they progressed.

They rounded a turn; the walls of the cavern fell away until they were invisible on either side. At the same instant a great gust of wind came tearing past and extinguished the torch.

"Hold it!" Hatfield told Uncle Mike, and fumbled for a match. He crept forward cautiously a few feet and abruptly glanced upward.

Far, far above was light. A narrow ragged strip of blue sky seemed to press directly down upon the broken crests of two awful cliffs that soared upward for at least twice a thousand feet. Feebly, reluctantly, the light filtered down into the vast gulf, but only the faint shadow-dregs, murky, uncertain. It changed the all-pervading gloom to a misty gray that was ghostly and faintly ominous.

Hatfield saw now that they stood on the brink of a frightful chasm. Its lip was jagged and torn, as if in some far distant age the mountain had been rent by some appalling convulsion of nature. Its depth he could not guess, for only a few feet below the lip the gloom was intense, nor could he see the far wall, which likewise was shrouded in darkness.

Cautiously he kicked a loose stone over the edge. It fell silently, and vanished. He listened, straining his ears, but no sound drifted up from the dark depths. They were so tremendous that the sound of the heavy rock striking bottom did not carry back, if it ever did strike bottom!

Hatfield had a feeling that this mighty wound in her breast, this terrific slash of an avenging angel's sword, sank to earth's very heart. He shook to the blasts of wind that tore down the gulf, his ears rang with its hum and roar.

"Good gosh, this is awful!" bawled Uncle Mike, wiping cold sweat from his face with a trembling hand.

Hatfield, his eyes becoming accustomed to the dim light, peered forward. He could dimly make out a ledge of rock, only a few feet in width, that soared upward from the lip of the gulf in a steep curve. Right out over the yawning blackness stretched the narrow curved ribbon, its upper surface slightly rounded. Under the blows of the rushing wind it hummed like a giant tuning fork of stone.

"It's a bridge," Hatfield shouted to Shaw, "a nacheral bridge that reaches to the other side of this hole, 'less I'm a heap mistook. Reckon we'll hafta cross it."

"Cross on *that?*" wailed Uncle Mike. "It might fall down, and even if it don't we'll be blowed off shore for certain."

"Guess we'll hafta risk it," Hatfield shouted back. "I figger it won't fall, and I reckon we won't get blowed off if we are careful. We'll hafta creep along in the dark. I've tried to light the torch, but there isn't a chance in this wind."

Uncle Mike squawked a despairing curse, but edged along behind Hatfield as the Texas Ranger set his foot cautiously upon the sloping surface of the bridge.

Foot by foot they crept along, leaning against the gusts of wind that tore down the gulf, cautiously testing each step as they advanced. The gloom was intense, deepening as the sun sank lower and less light seeped into the chasm. The bridge hummed and vibrated, seeming to jerk and sway as the blast beat upon it. They ceased to climb and reached a level space. They were at the very apex of the bridge, the frightful depths below them, the walls of rock towering above their heads. They paused for breath.

Without warning a strange and wonderful thing happened. A great sword of reddish flame pierced the gloom, falling full upon the bridge, staining the whirling mist wreaths in the gulf with bloody light. It was a beam from the setting sun, falling through some rift or crevice in the rock wall far above. Instantly what had been deepest shadow pulsed with intense light.

Hatfield could see that the soaring arch upon which they stood was comparatively slight. The thickness of the stone at the apex could not be more than a yard, perhaps less. The rock thickened at each end, however, as it approached the cliffs, until it was a mighty buttress welded to the solid mass of the wall.

At the far end of the bridge, twice a score of yards distant, he could see the dark opening which was a continuation of the cave.

"Quick!" he exclaimed to Uncle Mike. "Quick, while the light lasts. It'll be gone in a minute!"

They shuffled down the far slope of the bridge, stepped thankfully onto firm ground once more and turned to look back at the awesome scene.

For several minutes the great ray of light flamed and pulsed through the shadows, then as abruptly as it came it snapped off. Darkness, intense, impenetrable, closed down.

Hatfield stepped into the cave mouth.

Sheltered from the blast of the wind, he relighted the torch and they continued their progress.

"Well," grunted Uncle Mike Shaw, "I allus figgered I'd end up in hell, but I never 'spected to get a glimpse at the front door 'fore my time."

"Looked sorta like that, didn't it," chuckled Hatfield, "but it wasn't so bad as it looked. That bridge was firm enough."

"Coupla good licks with a sledge hammer would knock it down in the middle," grunted Shaw. "Weren't more'n a coupla feet thick all the twenty feet of that level stretch and for another ten foot down the far slope. Looked almighty flimsy to me when I was standin' on it lookin' down in that red light."

Hatfield nodded but directed his attention ahead. "Look," he suddenly exclaimed. "We shore aren't the fust jiggers to travel this road."

Cut deeply in the rock was a singular device. Old Mike stared at it, swore under his breath.

"What the blankety-blank-blank is it?" he demanded.

Hatfield examined the engraving with glowing eyes.

"It's a heraldic device," he explained.

"And 'less I'm a heap mistook, it's the lions and towers of Castile, from which developed the Spanish coat of arms. Leon was joined with Castile centuries ago, before the joining of Aragon and Castile produced modern Spain, and Leon adopted the arms of Castile."

"And that means?" hesitated Uncle Mike, understanding very little of what the Texas Ranger said.

"Can't say for shore," Hatfield replied, "but this cutting is mighty old and I'd say was done by or by the orders of that old Don Enrique de Leon, who was murdered by de Castro for the treasure they both knew about."

Old Mike wet his suddenly dry lips with the tip of his tongue.

"Then — then," he mumbled, "mebbe there really *is* a treasure!"

"Mebbe," Hatfield agreed tersely. "Let's go and see."

They continued down the passage, which was much more difficult to travel than that which led to the chasm and the bridge, due to the multitude of boulders and shattered rocks, between which were deep crevices in which it would be easy to break a leg. The air was close and heavy and they sweated profusely and suffered much from thirst.

"If there is anythin', we shore are earnin' it," croaked Uncle Mike. "Look, ain't that another of them markin's?"

It was. Again cut deeply into the rock wall was the shape of a shield adorned with lions and towers. And cut beneath it was a cross.

"I've a notion we're gettin' hot!" exclaimed Uncle Mike.

Another score of paces and the tunnel suddenly opened into a chamber of some extent. Hatfield lighted a fresh torch and held it high.

"Good gosh!" gasped Uncle Mike. "What's them things?"

His face stern, Hatfield walked across the room and bent a somber gaze upon the pitiful remains crouched against the rock, the shrunken ankle of each still fettered by a heavy chain.

"Injuns!" muttered Uncle Mike. "In this dry air they turned into mummies. Jest some dried skin stretched over bone. Yaquis, from the look of 'em."

"Yes," Hatfield said softly, "some of 'those dark ones who died toiling in the black dark'!"

Grimly he quoted the words written in blood by long dead Fernando de Castro. "And over there," he added, his voice cold, depressed, "is why they died."

Uncle Mike Shaw followed his gesture and stared pop-eyed at the rows of stacked metal bars. In the light of the torch they gave off a dull, smoldering glow. The old man shuffled over to them, lifted one from its place with evident effort.

"Gold," he muttered, "gold ingots! The produce of the mine when the gravel was a sight richer than what we turn up today. They hid it here until they could take it safe to Mexico and mebbe to Spain."

"Uh-huh," Hatfield agreed. "They used the Indians to carry it here, then chained them to the wall and left them to die in the dark, so they could never tell anybody where the gold was hidden. Salty gents in those days, old-timer! But the secret came down through the years by means of old de Castro's message, and mebbe other ways, too. 'Pears old Ramon Penelosa knew something about it, and figgered out how to get it, too, perhaps."

"But he never got it!" exulted Mike Shaw. "We've got it! Hatfield, we're rich!"

The Lone Wolf gazed at him, and in the flickering light of the torch his eyes were kind, and a trifle amused.

"You're rich," he corrected. "The gold is on yore claim, and it belongs to you, and Joe Hayes. There isn't as much value as old

301

de Castro figgered it in his day, but there's plenty to have you both sitting pretty, no matter how Escondida pans out."

He stemmed old Mike's torrent of protest with a raised hand and a finality in his voice that forbade further argument.

"I've got my job," he stated, "one that'll keep me busy for so long as I last, and I haven't got time to be burdened with a lot of *dinero*. Come on, now, let's get back. We can't carry it out by ourselves. Mighty few torches left and we don't want to get caught in the dark."

Old Mike stared into his lean, stern face, bewilderment struggling with admiration in his eyes, but without protest he turned and followed him up the passage. Weary, thirsty, depressed by the remembrance of the agonized lines in the faces of the Indians who had died of hunger and thirst in the black dark, they struggled toward the outer air.

They were not far from the cave mouth, and the bridge, clattering noisily over the boulders, their torch flaring and winking in the dark, when the air trembled to a sullen boom followed by a rending, crashing sound.

"Good gosh!" exclaimed Uncle Mike, "what in thunderation was that?"

Hatfield halted in his tracks, hesitated a

moment, then raced forward, his face grimly set, instinctively extinguishing the torch as he reached the cave mouth.

A pale shimmer, evidently of moonlight, seeped down from the vast heights. Through it the wind howled. The bridge hummed as before, but it seemed to Hatfield that the note had changed, was shrill, discordant, like to the dissonance of a broken harp string.

Cautiously he stepped upon the sloping surface, glided up it a few paces, and halted. Where the curve had formerly joined the level crest was a ragged edge of shattered stone. Before him stretched a gap, the width of which he could not guess, but so great that what lay beyond was shrouded in impenetrable gloom.

And as Hatfield stared in unbelieving bewilderment, from the black dark screeched maniacal laughter, then a jeering, exultant voice.

"Trapped!" yelled the voice above the roar of the wind. "Trapped, damn you! Stay there, you accursed meddler. Stay there until your bones are white! You came in search of gold? And found it? Fine! Eat it! Drink it! Soon you'd barter it all for a mouthful of water. Stay there with the gold you found! I am in no hurry. I will wait, and step over your bones when I come to get the gold!"

A last wild screech of laughter. Hatfield thought he heard the sound of retreating footsteps as the wind lulled for a moment. Then silence descended, silence as lonely and impenetrable as the black dark.

CHAPTER 31
A DARKENED TOMB

Cautiously Uncle Mike Shaw crept up the curving stone to join Hatfield.

"Good gosh!" he quavered, "who was it?"

"That isn't important now, not to us," Hatfield told him grimly, "and it may never be, from the looks of things."

"But what's it all about? What happened?"

"I was right back there in the treasure chamber, when I said the secret of this place might come down through the years by other ways besides old de Castro's letter. It did come down, and somebody figgered it out. I'd oughta thought of that, took it in account when the real meaning of that reflected ray of light come to me," he added with bitter self-accusation.

"That hellion had the key, and was just waiting for the right time of the year to use it. He come looking like we did, saw us working down the slope and bided his time. Chances are he knew about what he would find once he got in the cave. Slipped along after us, shoved a stick of dynamite into a crevice after we had passed over and blew down that thin section of the bridge. I'd shore oughta figgered on somebody mebbe having an eye on us."

"You ain't God Almighty, son; you can't be 'spected to think of everythin'. Wonder why he didn't just wait over there and shoot us as we crossed over. That'd been easy."

"It wouldn't suit his kind and blood," Hatfield replied. "He'll get a lot more pleasure outa thinking of us over here in the dark, starving and dying of thirst. That's what he meant when he told us to eat and drink gold. And he had to hang around and wait until he had a chance to taunt us 'fore he left. He could see our torch coming down the passage a long time 'fore we got here and cut his fuse accordingly. Yeah, he hadda stay and laugh. But I didn't hear no drums this time," he added cryptically.

Uncle Mike stared at him, but was too overwhelmed by their awful predicament to ask questions.

"I'm so thirsty right now I could chew leather," he muttered.

Hatfield stared into the dark. "We gotta figger us a way outa this mess," he declared, and added with grim certainty: "If we don't there'll be another corpse layin' somewhere in the hills within the next forty-eight hours with its tongue cut out!"

Vainly he tried to pierce the gloom beyond the broken edge. He quickly decided that the distance was too great to jump, even if he could see anything to land on.

"We've gotta know how far it is to the other broken end," he told Uncle Mike. "Take off yore coat and make a little tent with it. Then mebbe we can get one of these stalks burning good and toss it over when the wind lulls. Get a glimpse of what's over there, mebbe, 'fore it goes out."

They got the torch going after considerable difficulty. Taking advantage of a moment of comparative calm, Hatfield hurled the flaming stalk across the gulf. By the brief illumination before gusts extinguished the flame, he located the shattered end of the span on the far side of the gap. It was full forty feet distant and half of that lower down than the broken lip upon which they stood.

Old Mike's voice sounded hollowly through the dark. "Son, it looks like we're done. You never could jump that."

Hatfield did not reply. He fingered the thin strong lariat looped over his shoulder.

"If there was just something over there to

drop a loop over, it would be easy. The twine's plenty strong to hold me, to hold both of us, for that matter, and we could make a bridge of it and go 'crost hand over hand. But there's not a knob or projection over there, nor anything to tie to on this side, for that matter."

For a long time he stood staring into the dark, visioning the shattered fragment still projecting from the parent rock.

"It's a lot lower down than where we are, and that would help in a jump," he told Shaw.

"Son," protested the oldster, "you can't jump no forty feet through the dark, and you ain't gonna try it so long as I can holt onto you."

"No," Hatfield admitted, "I can't jump it, but I might swing 'crost on the end of the rope."

"Where you gonna tie to on this side?" demanded Shaw. "There ain't nothing above us but about a million miles of air, and down below —"

Hatfield's exultant exclamation interrupted him.

"You hit it, Uncle Mike," he shouted against the roar of the wind. "That's it — down below. Look, we can whip both ends of the rope over this busted section here, tie fast and make a swing of the loop that'll hang down below the under surface of the bridge. Then I can shin down the rope, stand in the loop and pump till I get her swinging way out toward the other broken end of the bridge. When I swing out as far as possible, I'll let go and the momentum will shoot me through the air and I'll land on the bridge over there. It's a cinch."

"You're loco!" howled Uncle Mike. "You'll go into the gulf shore as shootin'! If you don't you'll break your neck when you come down on the rock!"

"No I won't," Hatfield reassured him. "This broken end of the bridge is right in line with the one over there, and the rope will swing in a straight line. The rope's sixty feet long, and when I let go, I'll not be far above the surface of the bridge over there, which isn't more'n twenty feet lower than this end."

"But you can't do it in the dark," protested Uncle Mike. "If the rope should twist just a mite while you were swinging, you wouldn't know it and then you'd miss that narrer strip of rock over there."

Hatfield nodded. "You're right," he agreed thoughtfully. "I'll hafta have light, and we can't keep a torch going in this wind."

For a moment there was blank silence,

then Hatfield again exclaimed exultantly.

"The ray of light! The ray that stabs through the dark at sunset! It lights the whole place up like day. That's it, but we'll hafta wait until sunset."

Uncle Mike glanced upward toward the far-off strip of sky.

"Can't see no stars any more, and the sky's getting light," he announced. "Must be mighty nigh to mawnin'. We'll have all day to wait. Can tell when it's just about sunset by the looks of the sky. It'll be a long wait."

"Let's get the rope tied good and proper," Hatfield said cheerfully. "We want everything to be ready when it's time for the big show to come off."

Securing the rope to the narrow, thin jut of rock was not particularly difficult, and when the double strand dangled in the darkness, Hatfield was satisfied that it was long enough and would perform satisfactorily. After that there was nothing to do but retire to the cave mouth and wait for sunset.

The day seemed endless, tortured as they were by hunger and thirst, but finally its weary length drew to a close. The strip of sky grew darkling, tiny flecks of rose-colored cloud told that sunset was near at hand. Hatfield flexed his long arms, limbered his legs and stepped to the very lip of the broken bridge. As he did so a gnarled old hand reached through the gloom.

"Good luck, son," Uncle Mike Shaw said, a trifle unsteadily. "If you make it, I'll loosen one end of the rope and toss it over to you and you can hold it while I slide across. If you don't — well, wait for me on the 'other side.' I won't be far behind you!"

Hatfield returned the strong grip, and slid down the rope. He fixed his feet firmly in the loop and began to gently pump back and forth as he had done in a swing in boyhood days. His body began to sway backward and forward.

The rope creaked under his weight, the knots slipped and tightened. All about him was stygian gloom, through which the gusts of wind shrieked and howled, plucking at his clothes, buffeting him, seeking to hurl him into the bottomless depths.

It was a weird, awful position. He lost his sense of direction and could not tell for sure if he were swinging back and forth in a straight course beneath the arch of the bridge or veering sideways and out of line with the shattered tip far across the black gulf. Above him, Uncle Mike shouted hoarse encouragement.

Without the slightest warning came the

ray, cleaving through the dark like a fiery sword. Instantly the whole scene was illumined. Hatfield saw the ragged lip of the further fragment of the span. He was swinging to the full length of the twin ropes, but it seemed far, far away, and far below him. He set his jaw grimly, tried not to look into the horrible depths, freed his feet from the loop and, as the rope swung back, slipped down and hung by his hands.

Back, back he swung, until his rigid body almost touched the under surface of the span. Then he rushed forward at frightful speed. At the climax of the swing, his body standing straight out from the loop, he let go.

The wind howled in his ears, the mists swirled about him like a bloody shroud; and even as his body hurtled toward the narrow rounded surface of the broken bridge, the light ray snapped off as if sliced by a giant screen.

It seemed to Hatfield that he rushed through the awful dark for untold ages, the wind screeching past. For a terrible, paralyzing instant of time he "knew" he had veered sideways and missed the narrow rib of stone. Then, with a crash that set every joint to creaking, he struck the rounded surface. Red lights stormed before his eyes, he skittered, rolled, clutching with despairing fingers at the uneven surface. On the very lip of the stone he halted, and lay gasping.

Old Mike was howling anguished questions through the dark. Hatfield raised his head and roared back assurance. Shaw yelled like a Comanche at a scalping, his voice cracking on a joyous note.

Hatfield got painfully to his feet, decided that all joints were in working order and no bones broken. He shouted to Shaw to untie one end of the rope and throw it across. A moment later he heard it smack sharply against the stone nearby. He groped to where the end lay, seized it and drew the rope taut. He took a couple of turns about his waist, seated himself with his heels braced against a ridge of stone and shouted okay to Shaw. He felt the rope sag as Shaw put his weight upon it, but the oldster was a small man and much worn by the years.

Hatfield had little difficulty in holding the rope fairly taut. Shaw came sliding down through the darkness hand over hand. In a moment he was safe beside the Texas Ranger. Without wasting time in mutual congratulation at their almost miraculous escape from dreadful death, they hurried to the outer air.

They found the horses where they had left

them, saddled up and rode swiftly down the dark trail to town. They reached the Escondida building unobserved and old Mike dispatched a trusted swamper to round up Ted Harper. Soon the foreman came hurrying in, his eyes wide with astonishment.

"Good gosh!" he sputtered. "Where did you come from, boss? We thought — there's been talk —"

"No time for talk now," Hatfield rapped at him. "Get twenty of yore best fighting men together — with guns and horses. They'll be sworn in as a sheriff's posse. Send Casey to find Neal King and bring him here. Deputy Neal King, mind you, *not* Sheriff Wagner. Tell nobody you have seen us, and tell Casey to keep *his* mouth shut. And send that swamper out for all the coffee and chuck he can carry!"

Chapter 32
From North and South

There was an exultant trio grouped at a table in Ruby's saloon. Henry Lyons was there, and Sheriff Walt Wagner, and scar-faced Frank Durade. Heads close together, they talked in low tones, chuckling from time to time as do men over a satisfactorily finished task.

At the far end of the bar, young Joe Hayes talked earnestly with Ruby, who kept shaking her golden head. "You can't make me believe Hatfield has run off with anybody's money, or did anything underhanded," Ruby declared stubbornly.

Young Joe threw out his hands in expostulation, his face was worried, uncertain.

"*I* ain't tellin' you anythin', Ruby," he said. "I'm just passin' on what's bein' talked all over town. Hatfield and Uncle Mike was seed, just about daybreak yesterday, ridin' fast up the Chisos Trail, like they was headed for Welch. They never got to Welch.

Cyamon Johnson left Welch early yesterday headed for Coma. He didn't pass 'em on the way here, and there ain't no other way to get to Welch. They turned off somewhere, and about the only place you can turn off to from the Chisos is Mexico. Nobody knows what shape the Escondida 'fairs are in, but I'm scairt they're mighty bad."

"Something terrible has happened to Hatfield and Uncle Mike," Ruby insisted. "They wouldn't — good heavens!"

The swinging doors had suddenly flung open. Through them strode two tall figures. One was Deputy Sheriff Neal King, who sauntered toward the bar. The other, taller, broader, with eyes that were like pools of fire under ice, strode straight to the table at which were seated Lyons, Wagner and Durade, their faces blanched, staring as if at a ghost risen from the dead.

On the broad breast of the tall man gleamed a silver star set on a silver circle. It caught the light as he halted before the table and blazed as with leaping flame.

"Good gosh!" Walt Wagner squealed. "That feller's a ranger."

"Yeah, you sidewinders!" boomed Neal King. "A ranger! And — the *Lone Wolf!* Ever hear tell of him?"

Every man in that crowded room had.

They stared in awed wonder at the almost legendary figure who was discussed, admired and yarned about from end to end of Texas — and beyond — wherever fighting men got together.

Jim Hatfield's voice rang out, edged with steel, vibrating power and authority.

"In the name of the State of Texas, I arrest for robbery and murder, Walter Wagner, Frank Durade, and Enrique de Leon de Penelosa!"

Walt Wagner uttered a thin wail of terror. Durade shrank back, stiffened with set purpose. But at the utterance of the final name, Henry Lyons' somber face shone dark as death. His lips writhed back from his gleaming teeth, his eyes spat black flames. With a move too fast for the eye to follow, he hurled the heavy table over and crouched behind it, his heavy six leaping to his right hand.

Durade was on his feet, both hands held high above his head, as if in surrender.

"Not this time, Wilfred Crane!" Hatfield shouted as "Durade's" hands flashed downward in the deadly gambler's draw.

With the stubby derringers from his cunning sleeve holsters flaming in his hands, Wilfred Crane, known in the Big Bend country as Durade, died with Hatfield's bullets laced through his heart.

Walt Wagner dived for the door, but Neal King clubbed him to the floor with a slashing blow of his gun barrel. From behind the table, Henry Lyons shot it out with the ranger. A red streak leaped across Hatfield's bronzed cheek, one sleeve was slashed to ribbons by whining slugs, blood dripped from where one grazed his arm. He glanced about the panic-stricken saloon, slowly holstered his smoking guns and walked to the splintered table top.

Behind it lay Henry Lyons, who had been Don Enrique de Leon de Penelosa, in whose veins ran the blood of that stern old soldier and friend of the Spanish king whose name he bore.

Escolita, the little dancer, was sobbing in Ruby's arms, Joe Hayes hovering miserably nearby. Hatfield walked over to her.

"What was he to you?" he asked gently, motioning toward the dead Lyons.

"He was my stepfather," she replied, "the grandson of Ramon Penelosa. He married my mother, who was his cousin and, like him, of the blood of de Leon and de Penelosa. She died because of his cruelty and neglect. He came here nearly a year ago; and," she added quite simply, "I followed him to avenge my mother."

Hatfield nodded. "You knew about the story of the hidden gold of de Leon?"

The girl nodded. "The story has always been known in my family. There was an old paper that nobody could understand."

"Enrique — Lyons figgered it out," Hatfield said grimly. "That's why he came here. That, and to be revenged on the descendants of the man who murdered his grandfather. He did for Bruce Ralston, and others. You were next on the list, Hayes."

"No! No!" gasped Escolita.

Hatfield smiled a little, his eyes suddenly sunny. They hardened immediately, however, as they lighted on Walt Wagner sitting up and looking very sick.

"Bring him over here, Neal," he called.

When Wagner stood before him, downcast and trembling, Hatfield spoke to the point.

"Better talk, Wagner," he advised. "Yore two sidekicks are done in and Ted Harper and a special sheriff's posse are riding down the valley to drop a loop on the *Indians*."

"The Indians?" gasped Ruby.

"Uh-huh," Hatfield told her. "Lyons brought an outfit with him from Mexico. They are all asleep in Lyons' bunkhouse, with the dye washed off their faces and some of them with their black hair parted and combed as it should be. And those who haven't got black hair are not wearing their wigs. There won't be no more drums beating in the hills.

"It was the hair that gave me my fust notion of what was going on," he continued. "That jigger I shot over in Talking Water Canyon, the one who started the avalanche, had his hair combed down over his forehead, Yaqui style. But I figgered it sorta funny that there'd be the mark of a side part showing plain when his hair fell back. I looked close, then, and saw his face stained brown with vegetable dye any old-timer of the hills knows how to make. I've used it myself.

"The feller who died from the dynamite explosion that night on the old gold road was fixed up similar, and the other jigger that died was a red-headed white man, sorta funny company for a band of raiding Yaquis."

"But what about the Injun drums?" demanded Uncle Mike Shaw, who had joined the group at the end of the bar.

"You'd oughta know better, old-timer" Hatfield chided. "I've had considerable experience with Indians, and I never knew them to go round beating drums promiscuous-like when anything happened. Drums are serious business with Indians and are beat only on important and extra special occasions. The drums were to make folks *think* Indian, and blame Indians for what was happening. Worked pretty well.

"I learned that Durade had once worked for Lyons. Lyons pretended to have a row with him and fired him, and sent him to get in with Joe Hayes and egg him on to doing things which would sooner or later cast suspicion on Joe. I was sorta uncertain about Joe at fust, myself. He was allus around when things happened, but then so was Lyons.

"Funny thing, how owlhoots manage to tangle their own rope," he added, his green eyes brooding. "Crane went all the way in his character of Durade, the gambler he usta be when he formerly associated with Lyons, 'fore he mixed in the banking business and turned respectable, for a while. He bleached his naturally black hair, grew a beard and bleached that, too.

"If you look close at the roots, you'll see the dark hair coming through. Way back in the Guadalupes, months ago, when I had a shooting with Crane and he got away, I must have shot his eye out and give him that scar. That with his bleached hair and whiskers changed him until he just wasn't recognizable as Crane.

"But when he posed as a Yaqui with the rest of the outfit, he went whole hawg again — put on a black wig, stained his bleached whiskers with an Indian dye that's easy to wash off and stuck a glass eye in his empty socket. Nobody would recognize him as Durade in that getup; but when he did that, *he turned himself back into Wilfred Crane again,* and that night when the dynamite exploded on the gold road, I spotted him for Crane. Still, though, I hadn't tied him up with Durade."

"How did you do it?" asked old Mike.

"Didn't do it until tonight," Hatfield admitted. "When he threw his hands up, it was just the same gesture Crane used when he made the gambler's draw on me the first time we got together. I had to let him know I had him hawgtied 'fore he cashed in. He had recognized me all along as the man he had a run-in with, but Crane never knew me for a Texas Ranger, otherwise they mighta tried even harder than they did to cash me in."

Hatfield turned suddenly to Wagner. "Lyons killed the sheriff, didn't he?"

"Yes," Wagner admitted. "He stood outside the window and heard you talking to Dobson and saw you give him that thirty-two-twenty gun. Bruce Ralston grabbed that gun off Lyons the night Lyons and the outfit was torturin' him back in Yaller Hoss Canyon. Killed a man who was holdin' him and broke away; but Lyons drilled him as he rode off.

"Lyons hadda get that gun back and do for Dobson — there's folks in the valley knowed he carried it. If he'd had any notion you was a ranger 'stead of jest a jigger hornin' into the game, he'd tried harder to do you in. You fooled everybody, Hatfield."

"How'd you come to ketch onto Lyons in the fust place?" old Mike asked.

"His name," the Lone Wolf replied. "Henry Lyons is a free translation of the Spanish Enrique de Leon. Seems owlhoots have a habit of taking aliases that are similar in some way or other to their real names. I got to thinking serious on the revenge angle when you told that yarn about the Howard-Penelosa feud.

"Bruce Ralston had his tongue cut out, and so did that XT cowboy who was a cousin to him, and I found out that feller Warner who was hung on a chola cactus was related to old John Howard, and *his* tongue was cut out, you'll rec'lect. But that didn't happen to the other XT puncher, who wasn't of the Howard clan. He jest had the bad luck to be with the other one Lyons

323

was after when the gang caught him. 'Cording to the story, Don Ramon Penelosa's tongue was cut in two by John Howard's bullet and he couldn't give his son the last message he was trying to.

"They remember things like that down in *mañana* land. Don Ramon Penelosa's son never made it back into Texas to avenge the killing of his father, but he told *his* son, Enrique de Leon de Penelosa, and swore him to carry on the feud. Sounds funny, hate carrying down that way through the years — but, well my own family fought for fifty years with another family back in Kentucky and Virginia — a fight that started over the killing of a pig!

"Then Lyons come into the bar here the first night I saw Escolita, and I saw she was scairt stiff of him. That was funny, seeing as she just recent come from down Mexico way and Lyons had been here nearly a year. He tried to kidnap her that night. I learned Lyons was in town the night the girl Flame was knifed in the hallway outside of Escolita's room. Lyons had figgered what Escolita was up to and set out to cash her in."

Escolita shuddered and nodded her black head vigorously. Hatfield paused to roll a cigarette.

"But where Lyons slipped bad," he continued, "was with the cartridge loops on his gun belt. Those loops were originally built to hold thirty-two-twenty cartridges. When he got rid of that odd-calibred gun, instead of getting a new belt, he just opened out the loops a mite to accommodate forty-five calibre shells. Mighty careless, for the marks of the original stitching showed if you looked close. The rest was easy."

"Uh-huh," grunted Uncle Mike Shaw, "easy as ketchin' rattlesnakes with yore bare hands! But why did Lyons start makin' trouble for me and the mine?"

"He was scairt you might uncover the hiding place of the de Leon gold when you started tearing down the gravel bank with water," Hatfield explained. "He knew it was up there somewhere on the slope, but couldn't tell for shore just where until the ray of light revealed it."

Suddenly he turned to Escolita, smiled down at her.

"Well, *señorita,*" he said, "isn't it about time you and Joe stopped fighting and got together?"

Hayes looked perfectly willing, but the girl resolutely shook her head.

"No, no," she exclaimed. "He is one of the family my family hates!"

Hatfield reached out, cupped her white

325

little chin in his bronzed hand. She stared up at him with wide eyes. Slowly, distinctly, he quoted the words cut in the granite face of the Devil's Finger.

"Heard that before, haven't you?" he asked softly.

"*Si, si!*" she replied in surprise. "It is cut in the stone of a great cliff that stands between two streams near my home in *Mejico*. How know you the words?"

"Lyons cut them in that big spire up there," he replied, gesturing toward the Finger. He reached out and grasped Joe Hayes' hand. Slowly he drew it and the girl's together.

"The stream of the North and the stream of the South," he quoted softly, and placed the two hands together. "Let them join, and blood will cease to cry out for blood. That's the way to end feuds — a feller can't very well fight with his wife's relations!"

"Well, they're shore joined close enough now," remarked Uncle Mike as Joe Hayes clasped her in his strong arms and Escolita offered no objection.

Hatfield smiled down at them, turned to Ruby, who was gazing at him with eyes that seemed to look out of a past that was dead. He took her hand and bowed over it courteously.

"Reckon I'll be riding now," he said. "Captain McDowell has another little chore for me over east. Goodbye, ma'am, reckon the next time I happen this way, you'll sorta be a grandmother by adoption!"

Through the pale radiance of the dying moon he rode the Chisos Trail, lounging in his saddle with careless grace, toward where new and stirring adventure waited, pleasant anticipation in his green eyes. No drums beat in the shadow of the hills, no flying hoofs of terror pounded the dusty trail.

But far up in the lonely fastness of the Phantoms sounded the beautiful wild mourn of a hunting wolf.